Kodiak

#1 Trial By Fire

by

Matt Waterhouse

Other stories in the

Kodiak universe:

Red Saints (2017)

The Eye Of The Universe (2020)

Matt Waterhouse

Thank you to all who support me in my writing.

Lee and Karl, love you guys.

My family, for their support.

Alexander Lidström, for bringing the Kodiak to life.

The many authors and artists
on Minds, for the inspiration and
fun times.

Kodiak 1: Trial By Fire

1

U rsa Patrol Squadron moved along the border that had cut the

Procyon star system in half, flying in a tight formation. The four Dart-Class corvettes stayed within two kilometres of each other, their sensor pulses dancing over the void, searching for any sign of a ship straying stealthily across into the space controlled by the Sol Fleet.

The enemy was cunning and brutal in equal measure, and the Sol Fleet had paid the price for carelessness many times. For a religion seemingly bound by truth, kindness, empathy and compassion, The Church Of The Whole had a duplicitous side to them that rivalled the slipperiest of serpents.

Fully aware of this, Lieutenant Orson Grant stared at the tactical sensor screens, the blanket of fatigue drooping around his shoulders as the gunship's terrible coffee started to wear off. All four of the EDSV Kodiak's rapid-fire vulcan rail turrets were poised, with hyper-velocity rounds loaded into both of their heavy-duty, forward-facing rail cannons. He glanced over at Lieutenant Rosario Diaz, the ship's communications officer, sitting beside him.

"Any word from the rest of the patrol?"

"The Arctos and the Grizzly picked up the same signals we did about ten minutes ago. They're keeping an eye on them, but it looks more like a sensor ghost than a ship."

"Hmm." Grant stifled a yawn. "It's like we're chasing shadows."

"I'll make that judgement, Lieutenant," Captain N'Koudou snapped from the command chair.

Grant glanced back at her, that same feeling of frustration he felt daily creeping over his tiredness. At the helm, Lieutenant Commander Winters smirked back at him. Grant turned back to the console, co-ordinating the Kodiak's sensor scans with the Martimus, the fourth ship in their patrol. They had been tracking the readings for most of the day, the potential for danger breaking through the monotony, but not enough for tensions on the ship to be anything but strained.

"The Martimus hasn't picked up anything for the last half hour either, Captain," Grant said. "The last thing of note aside from standard background noise was a class one comet half a parsec away."

"I shouldn't need to remind you that their ships have active jamming, Mr Grant," N'Koudou said dismissively.

"We'd still be able to see some sign of them, ma'am. Their jammers aren't perfect."

"I'm glad you have confidence in your abilities, Lieutenant, but I prefer to be thorough." She turned to face him for long enough to insert the knife. "Remind me the cost of not being thorough, Mr Grant?"

Grant gritted his teeth and glared around at her. She wasn't even looking at him, her eyes were on a report that had come in to the readout on her console. Diaz glanced at him, as did the rest of the bridge crew. Grant re-focused on the sensor scans, switching to a different frequency, signalling the Martimus to do the same.

"The Captain asked you a question, Mr Grant," Winters said.

"I'm aware of that, ma'am, and she knows my answer already. Running another set of scans now," Grant said, keeping his voice as neutral as he could. Diaz gave him a sidelong look, opening her mouth to say something, but seeming to think better of it.

"Diaz, transmit our sensor data to the Grizzly and the Arctos, let them know I'd like a second opinion from their tactical officers," N'Koudou said smoothly. "They should have checked your working by the time your shift starts again, Mr Grant."

Diaz's fingers danced over the console. "Scans transmitted and received, Captain."

"Good."

The lights in each corner of the bridge went from blue to green. "Speaking of which …" N'Koudou pressed her thumb to the intercom. "Alpha shift is up, time for changeover. Delta shift to the bridge."

Grant glanced at a review of the anomalies the patrol had picked up in the last eight hours. Nothing seemed out of the ordinary, but he wasn't about to allow himself to miss anything that could come back to bite them, not to mention something that would be held against him later.

"Saved by the bell, Grant," Winters muttered at him as she passed. Grant ignored her, focusing in on the echoes they had picked up. Diaz opened her mouth again, to double down or perhaps offer comfort, but Grant wanted none of it. He stopped her with a glare and a shake of his head. She looked away, and stood up as Crewman Holden entered the bridge to take the comm station. Crewman O'Hare replaced Winters at the helm, keying in to the navigational data from the rest of the squadron.

Someone tapped Grant on the shoulder, and he glanced around. The looming, pale face of Ensign Or'Veth looked down at him impassively. "Your shift is over, Lieutenant Grant," he sang in his musical, gentle voice.

"I know, I was just … checking my work."

"I see."

Grant sighed and stood up. The young Acamar crewman still towered over him. "We've been tracking a couple of anomalies on sensors. Could just be echoes, but they're worth keeping an eye on."

"I shall watch them carefully."

Grant nodded to him and left the bridge, stepping into the long corridor that led back towards the engine room. Despite the Kodiak's small crew, there was an element of hustle and bustle as Delta shift took their stations. He rubbed his eyes, heading for the access ladder that led to the other decks. His stomach growled at him, reminding him that he hadn't eaten since that morning. He stopped next to an intercom panel and pressed his thumb to the controls.

"Grant to Aarons."

The Chief Engineer's voice crackled over the speakers. "Aarons here."

"Fancy a bite to eat?"

"I'm headin' that way now. Meet ya there."

"Alright."

Grant signed out and carried on down the cramped corridor, brushing past another Acamar, the doctor, Shen'Zahr. She was a little more seasoned than Or'Veth, and a little more used to the emotion and chaos of humanity. They gave each other a nod as she walked towards sickbay, but no words passed between them.

When he reached the access ladder, Grant sighed. Winters was waiting for him, her arms folded. "Ma'am."

"Try not to question the Captain, Mr Grant," she said, her voice dripping with condescension as thick as honey. "It's not a good look."

Grant forced as genuine a smile as he could, but it still came out tight. "I wasn't questioning the Captain, Winters. I was giving her a report on sensor scans. There's a difference."

"If she wants a report, she'll ask for it. I don't remember her asking for it …" Her lip curled. "… and it's *Lieutenant Commander* Winters, by the way. You should know how to address a superior officer."

"If she's chasing wild geese it's my job to tell her, as the officer in charge of tactical operations."

"Not for much longer," Winters snapped. "You are very far from professional, Mr Grant."

"Speak for yourself, ma'am."

The XO's eyes narrowed. "In your time aboard this ship, you've been insubordinate and lacking in your duties. Make no mistake, you were forced on Captain N'Koudou by Sol Fleet Command, under the strange impression that you deserved some kind of second chance after what you did. If it were up to her, or up to me, you'd be a crewman on a garbage scow."

"Well, luckily for me, it wasn't up to you or her. Will that be all? I'm hungry, it was a long shift."

"Watch your tone, Grant."

Grant straightened up and stood to attention. "With all due respect, *Lieutenant Commander*, I've been trying to do my duty as weapons officer to the best of my abilities. No-one is more aware of my history than me. I've been aboard the Kodiak for almost a year, in more than twenty combat engagements. I have a duty to the safety of this ship and crew, and to every free human in this war. Last I checked, we're all still alive, which means that I'm at least competent, so your constant questioning of me is a waste of your valuable time and the captain's."

Winters stepped closer to him. "Do you have any idea how many reprimands are on your permanent record? Say another word. I dare you. Those ranking pips on your chest aren't fixed there. We can easily take them away."

Grant didn't let himself waver. "Way I see it, if you and the N'Koudou are anything to go by, my career is already in the toilet. Go ahead and demote me. I don't care about my rank at this point. This is a war. I care about keeping this crew alive."

Winters shook her head and snorted. "Maybe you should have cared about keeping the crew alive on the Berlin."

Grant gritted his teeth so hard he heard them creak. Winters studied his reaction for a moment, before taking hold of the access ladder. "Carry on, Lieutenant."

Grant waited as she descended to deck three, calming himself as best he could, waiting for the curses and slurs to peter out in his head. He'd known in the aftermath of the incident aboard the EDSV Berlin that there would be people who would never forget it, much less forgive his role in it. The knowledge of that made the constant reminders no easier.

When he had graduated from the Officer's Academy, he had thought he had some idea about the realities of the Interstellar Holy War that had been raging for decades. Even so, he could never have imagined the horrors of the last year, the massacre at Gargantua, the suicide attacks on colonies and space stations, the brutal breaking of every ceasefire that The Sol Fleet and Acamar had attempted to broker with The Church Of The Whole.

Grant swallowed his bitterness. Nothing he could do about any of that, aside from his duty aboard the Kodiak. He doubled back and headed towards the bunk room, in desperate need of one of the gunship's signature lukewarm showers, the storm from the memories of his own mistakes still raging in his head.

***

Diaz smiled as Winters joined her and Captain N'Koudou at the table, her tray of military rations clattering against the metal surface. This was the first time she had been called over to eat with the command crew, an honour that hadn't been bestowed on many other of the officers or enlisted personnel.

"Long day..." Winters muttered as she settled in her chair. "Long day, with a whole lot of nothing."

"No argument here," N'Koudou said with a grin. "But these patrols keep the Free Colonies safe."

"Yeah, yeah. The extranet reminds me every time I take a piss."

N'Koudou chuckled. "Well, we can set course for Earth in the morning, loaded for bear, if we don't see anything tomorrow." She turned to Diaz. "This is a long overdue dinner, Rosario."

Diaz smiled. "I wasn't counting, ma'am. I know you're both busy."

"Are we ever," N'Koudou snorted. "You may have guessed that this isn't a social call."

Diaz bit into her lukewarm ration bar, doing her best not to grimace at the taste, texture, and aftertaste. "I didn't have a guess either way, Captain."

"Right. Well, Lieutenant Commander Winters and I have been looking over the senior officers records, and yours stands out quite a bit."

"Thank you, Captain."

"When this patrol is finished, we'll be about a fortnight from the end of our tour of duty. We'll be sent out again, no doubt, but we're going to be making some changes. Winters is overdue a promotion to Commander, and we'll be in the market for a new second officer. You're on our shortlist."

Diaz opened her mouth in surprise. "I … wow … I'm …"

"It's down to you, Chief Aarons, and Doctor Shen'Zahr," Winters said. "We know you don't necessarily have their experience, but we'd like all of the command crew to be on the bridge in a crunch."

Diaz nodded, almost reluctant to ask her next question. "What about Lieutenant Grant? Does he know he's being replaced? He probably won't be happy about it."

N'Koudou sipped her coffee. "He's being transferred the moment we dock at the nearest port. I want a second officer I can rely on, and that isn't Grant. As for how he feels about it, I don't care."

Diaz was shocked at the Captain's bluntness, although she could have guessed that Grant was on the way out. She took another bite of her sub-standard dinner, unsure of what to say.

"We've got our reasons, Ro," Winters said. "It's not a decision we take lightly, but given his history …"

"I understand. The tension on the bridge is … to be honest, it's not easy to work with. People have noticed that he's never been in charge of a shift. If he's not there … it'll probably make things easier. Not that I have anything against him personally, he's never been any trouble to me, but …"

13

"You don't have to be so diplomatic with us, Lieutenant. A year of him at tactical has been more than enough, I just hope it'll be enough for the Admiralty." N'Koudou said. Her eyes were drawn to the door. "Ah. Speak of the devil, and he shall appear."

Diaz glanced over her shoulder. Grant had entered the cramped mess compartment, rubbing his eyes. He looked over at the three of them, met Diaz's gaze, then looked away quickly. He picked up a tray of rations from the dispenser and joined Chief Aarons at a table as far from the command crew as he could.

Diaz glanced at the Captain and XO, noting how cold they had become. "Can I ask a question, Captain?"

N'Koudou glanced at her. "Of course."

"What did he do?"

Both Winters and N'Koudou looked at her in surprise. "You haven't heard?" Winters asked.

"I've heard rumours, but everyone's story is completely different. Is he a defector, or an apostate, something like that?"

N'Koudou shook her head. "Nothing like that. This isn't his first ship. On one of his assignments on a heavy cruiser, he got half the crew killed."

Diaz gaped. "What?"

N'Koudou sighed. "Aboard the EDSV Berlin, you haven't heard about this?"

"Not the full story, no … but the name's familiar, now you mention it."

"Grant was the weapons officer. The ship was ambushed and crippled on a patrol by Whole ships. The captain and XO and most of the officers were killed. He was next in line for the big chair, so command passed to him … but he made a mistake."

"The Berlin's engines were heavily damaged," Winters continued. "They were operable, but he missed something. When the ship went to FTL, it was flooded with lethal levels of radiation before the seals could catch it. If he'd seen the malfunction, those people would be alive. The tribunal found him guilty of gross negligence, and he was demoted. If we weren't at war, he'd have been kicked out of the service, but he did time for it."

"How much time?"

Winters snorted. "Not enough."

"God." Diaz looked at Grant as he chatted to Aarons, as he occasionally glanced up at the Captain's table. "I mean … he can't have been that old at the time, that long out of the Academy … and he's not an engineer … maybe he just missed it."

"That's not how it works when you're the CO, even the acting CO," N'Koudou grunted. "The buck stops with you, you make the decisions. He made bad ones, and his crew paid the price."

Again, Diaz hesitated before she spoke. "I've heard … I mean, some of the crew were talking about a mutiny against him. They didn't mention which ship it happened on, but I guess they could have meant ..."

N'Koudou snorted. "A conspiracy theory. Grant has his supporters. Why do you think he's here, and part of the command crew no less?"

"I don't know ... all due respect, but the Kodiak isn't exactly a starship, not like the Berlin is."

"Easy how you talk about my ship, Lieutenant Diaz."

Diaz flushed. "Right, sorry ma'am."

N'Koudou sighed. "The decision to assign Grant here was taken over my head, and I'm going to rectify that. His poor record aboard the Kodiak can't be disputed." She looked at Diaz and smiled. "No great loss, but his loss could be your gain, if you play your cards right."

"I intend to play them more than right, Captain."

N'Koudou and Winters shared a smile. "Glad to hear it, Lieutenant," the captain said, patting her on the shoulder.

***

Aarons grimaced as he swilled the coffee around his mouth. "I'm tellin' you, Orson, if we don't get a re-supply soon, I'm gonna flip my shit."

Grant snorted. "What, you don't like hot mush and bad coffee?"

"Solid food, that's all I'm askin'. Somethin' I can actually chew."

Grant looked out of the viewport at the enemy's side of the line. "At least you haven't been chasing specks of grit on the sensor screen all bloody day."

"With how the Captain was carryin' on, you'd have thought we were huntin' the Red October."

"The what?"

Aarons rolled his eyes. "Doesn't matter. Watch more twentieth century video art. You sayin' it's nothing to worry about?"

"Shit, Dalian, we're practically tickling the border with The Whole out here. Everything is technically something to worry about, but we know what we're looking for at this point. We're worked up over nothing."

"Heh, if you say so. Will you stop looking at the ladies for a minute or two?"

Grant tore his eyes off the command table. "It's not what you think. I had another run in with Winters."

"Ah..."

"Now she's got her lips around Diaz's ear ... the one person on my bridge shift that doesn't speak to me with passive aggressiveness, or actual aggressiveness."

Aarons sighed. "That's the bed they made for ya, I guess. Stiff upper lip, my friend. It ain't anything new."

Grant grunted. "Right."

"Come on, finish your slop and put ya feet up."

"Fine, fine."

The Kodiak's intercom whistled. "Bridge to Captain N'Koudou."

Grant sighed, catching crewman Holden's tone on the transmission. "Great. That's just great."

N'Koudou got up and walked over to the input console on the wall.

"Go ahead, bridge."

"The squadron's been rerouted from our patrol. Our listening post in sector five picked up a distress call from the EDSV Potemkin, we've been ordered to intercept."

"Set course, and signal the rest of the squadron."

"Aye, Captain."

N'Koudou flicked two more buttons on the console. "Alert One, all hands to battle stations."

Everyone in the mess hall stood up at once and made for the door. Grant downed his coffee with a grunt, and patted Aarons on the shoulder. "No rest for the wicked, Chief. Let's get to it."

2

Grant took his position at the tactical console, signalling the

gunners of the four rapid-fire vulcan rail-gun turrets mounted on the Kodiak's prow, and the crewmen operating the two heavy rail cannons. He watched as his readouts lit up with the confirmation sign from each of the weapon banks. The maintenance scans confirmed that the Kodiak's armour was solid, the manoeuvring thrusters and stabilisers were fine. He began running diagnostics on the targeting sensors immediately.

"Offensive and defensive systems ready at your order, Captain," he said.

N'Koudòu barely nodded. "Diaz, what do we know about the Potemkin?"

"She's Independence Class, ma'am, Captain Fairbrand commanding. Recent assignment was a deep strike mission to Wolf 359, she was set to rendezvous with Battle Group Omega."

"Looks like they didn't make it," Winters muttered from the helm.

"Load the rail-guns, Mr Grant, I want antimatter rounds in the heavy cannons."

Grant sent the instructions on to the gunners. "Aye, captain."

"Diaz, signal the squadron. Winters, time to intercept?"

"Three minutes, Captain."

N'Koudou turned to Grant. "Can I bother you for some sensor scans, Lieutenant?"

Grant looked at the readouts. "Still nothing, Captain. I think we're being jammed, there's not enough interference in the area for it to happen naturally. I can cut through it, but I'll need a minute."

"Make it thirty seconds."

Grant glanced at Diaz. "Would you mind running the sensors through the main transmitters? We might isolate the frequency of their jammer a little faster."

Diaz nodded, and Grant switched them over, eliminating frequencies with one hand, keeping an eye on the sensor scans. Within twenty seconds, he had it. "The Potemkin has lost engines, but she's fighting with everything she's got. All her fighters are deployed, most have been destroyed. The Whole have got ... at least two Quinns on sensors, with more intermittent sensor readings. Smaller ships, running jammers. Corvettes, judging by the size, between six and ten. Probably fighters too."

"Increase speed, Winters," N'Koudou muttered. "Diaz, signal the squadron. I want every ship to come out of FTL speed firing."

"Twenty seconds," Winters said, her voice tense.

"Spin up the vulcans, Grant. Ready point-defence lasers."

"Yes, ma'am." The four vulcan guns began revolving, ammunition loaded and ready. He watched heavy-duty, hyper-velocity, antimatter rounds slide into the breaches of the two heavy cannons. The eighteen small laser turrets powered up, their proximity targeting sensors fully operational.

"Attack formation Shield Sigma," N'Koudou said, leaning forwards.

"The squadron has confirmed." Diaz said. "Martimus and Grizzly are on our flanks."

"Five seconds," Winters barked.

"Here we go," Diaz muttered.

The stars surged back into view as the Kodiak decelerated. The Potemkin was dead in space ahead of them, one of its FTL engines blown apart, chunks of its huge, bulky hull exposed to space. All of the stricken battleship's guns were firing, taking on the corvettes trying to flank them. A pair of The Whole's Quinn-Class cruisers were sweeping around it for an another pass. Their rail-gun blasts smashed into the Potemkin's weakened armour.

Grant locked all four vulcans on the lead Quinn, and they barked to life. The sound of the gatling guns was audible inside the ship as the vibrations shook the hull. Armour-piercing rounds lanced forward from each one, peppering the cruiser's hull.

The Martimus and Grizzly followed suit, opening fire with their rail-guns, and the Quinn banked away from the Potemkin, activating its jammers. The second cruiser spun towards them and opened fire with its broadside cannons, and Grant boosted power to the point defence systems.

A torpedo exploded close by as the PD lasers blasted it. The ship bucked as the shockwave kicked them, but everyone managed to stay at their stations.

"Armour holding!" Grant called.

"Captain, the Arctos has engaged a squadron of fighters," Diaz said urgently. Grant looked at his screens, spotting the engine flares off their port side.

"Confirmed," he said. "They're flanking us!"

"Pull up, Winters!" N'Koudou shouted. "Diaz, signal the Grizzly, tell them to engage those fighters with the Arctos! Grant, I need firing solutions on that cruiser!"

"You've got them, Captain."

"Then fire!"

The Kodiak arced upwards, and one of the corvettes manoeuvred to

Matt Waterhouse

follow them. Grant signalled the two ventral turrets to angle downwards, and peppered the second Quinn with rail-gun fire. With his left hand he boosted power to the aft PD lasers, and with his right he tracked the other cruiser, watching as the fluctuating sensor readings came about and started back towards the crippled battleship.

"Captain, that cruiser is making a direct run at the Potemkin," he called over his shoulder. Rail-gun fire from the pursuing corvette hit them hard, overwhelming their point defence, and some of his readouts flickered as the power fluctuated. "There's a corvette right on our ass!"

"Where's the Martimus?" N'Koudou shouted.

Diaz's fingers flew across her console. "She's got problems of her own, two more corvettes to starboard!"

The ship bucked again, and ahead of them the Quinn pointed its nose up towards them, its torpedo tubes open. "Captain!"

"Winters, dive on my mark, full power to thrusters!"

"Aye, Captain!"

The Quinn fired.

"Now!"

Winters pulled the Kodiak into sharp dive. One of the torpedoes passed them, the other exploded two hundred metres off their dorsal hull.

Kodiak 1: Trial By Fire

The Kodiak seemed to scream in pain under the force of the shockwave. Somewhere behind Grant, there was an explosion as the power conduits ruptured.

"Shit!" N'Koudou hissed, she hammered the intercom. "Medical emergency! Dr Shen'Zahr and Lieutenant Or'Veth to the bridge!"

Grant glanced back. Lauren White, who had been at the general operations console, was hanging half out of her chair, her body smoking and limp. The safety harness had kept her in place. Blood had spattered across the floor beside her, thin red streaks, with more pooling beneath her head.

"Captain, I've got both heavy cannons locked on the cruiser!" Grant said.

"Good for you," N'Koudou spat. "Winters, get our nose up and pointed at that bastard."

"Yes ma'am!"

"Did we shake that corvette?"

Grant glanced at the sensor readouts. "They're coming about, looks like that second torpedo grazed them. We're out of range, but that won't last long."

"One at a time, Grant," N'Koudou said through gritted teeth. The Kodiak's nose pointed at the cruiser's underbelly. "Fire at will."

Grant signalled the vulcans, and both the heavy rail cannons. The projectiles blasted through the Quinn's weakened armour and blew two large, burning holes in their engineering section. "Their power's fluctuating. Looks like we hit them in a tender spot."

"Congratulate yourself later, Grant. Damage report, Diaz."

Diaz's jaw tightened as she skimmed through the reports. "Sickbay confirms three dead. Dorsal armour's buckling. Superficial damage to the engine pod."

"Weapons?"

Grant glanced at his console. "Ammunition at eighty percent, nothing to worry about yet."

On the screen, the other Quinn fired on the Potemkin again, breaching its armour and striking the command deck. Winters struck the helm console in frustration.

"Diaz?" N'Koudou said urgently.

"Hold on..." Diaz typed for a moment, before sighing in relief. "I'm still in contact with Captain Fairbrand. The bridge crew relocated to auxiliary control when they lost engines. Most of the crew are holed up away from the outer hull."

"That corvette is about ten seconds from weapons range, Captain," Grant warned. On his screens, the Quinn engaged its jammer once more.

"Evasive manoeuvres, Winters. Diaz, can the Potemkin hold out?" N'Koudou demanded.

"Fairbrand thinks so, but Lieutenant Grant could confirm that."

Kodiak 1: Trial By Fire

Grant scanned the Potemkin, as Dr Shen'Zahr and Lieutenant Or'Veth ran onto the bridge. Shen'Zahr spotted White immediately and began tending to her with her emergency medical kit.

"Their armour is breached on all decks, their structural integrity systems are running at fifty percent. Almost all their PD systems are gone. They could survive another pass if they're lucky, but I wouldn't push it."

A high pitched whine came from Shen'Zahr's medical readouts, and she sighed, carefully unstrapping and lifting White's body from her station. Or'Veth took the operations station immediately. N'Koudou took a breath as the doctor lay the dead officer in the corner of the room, preparing to take her to sickbay on a collapsible stretcher.

"Come about, Winters," N'Koudou said gruffly. "How's the rest of the squadron, Diaz?"

"Everyone's taken some hits, but they're still flying, ma'am. The Arctos has lost power to their FTL drive, the Martimus is on emergency power."

The corvette came into view on Grant's scope, its weapons tracking them. It managed to get off a couple of shots before two of the Kodiak's heavy rail cannon slugs blew off one of its wings, and the vulcans sheared off the neck connecting the bridge section from the hull.

N'Koudou grinned. "Good shooting, Grant. Contact the Arctos, get them on our wing. Tell the Grizzly to cover the Martimus."

A large sensor distortion appeared on Grant's screens, approaching them. "Captain, it looks like that Quinn is closing on us."

"Auxiliary power to PD systems. Diaz, where's our support?"

"Another corvette has intercepted them, they're taking fire."

The cruiser matched their course, its cannons turning towards them.

N'Koudou leaned forwards. "Winters, swing around behind the …"

The deck lurched violently as the cruiser blasted the Kodiak in her port side. The rail-gun fire was relentless. The point defence lasers couldn't keep up with the sheer volume of hyper-velocity slugs slamming into them, and holes started to appear in the port armour. Grant gritted his teeth as screens around him began to short out and shatter, as signals from the lasers flickered and died. As he diverted more power to them from the auxiliary batteries, three heavy slugs breached their port side armour.

One of the maintenance ducts burst into flame at the rear of the bridge, and as his attention was pulled towards that, the torpedo alert sounded. N'Koudou was shouting something, but he couldn't hear her over the chaos. Grant diverted emergency power to the port lasers, all of it, and the impact of the exploding torpedoes kicked him so hard he felt the harness on his seat buckle.

There was a bright flash, then darkness. Grant's ears popped and started ringing. His back and shoulder screamed at him. The emergency lights began glowing softly, casting an eerie green glow over the room. Blearily, he spotted Diaz beside him at the comm station, sagging in her harness, unconscious. There was blood dripping from her nose and ears: decompression, but only for a moment. The hull had been breached, but the emergency seals had to be in place.

His ears felt like there were hot pokers sticking into them, but his hearing was beginning to return. The emergency alert was wailing all around him. He reached out to check Diaz's pulse, and her eyes snapped open. She jerked in her seat and looked up at him, confused for half a second, before her mind cleared. "Shit."

"Yeah," Grant grunted as he wiped the blood from his nostrils. His shoulder felt dislocated, but that could wait. He focused his eyes on the tactical station. The screens were either flickering or smashed. He managed to power one of them, calling up a damage report.

"Main power generator's offline, weapons too. Those torpedoes overloaded the point-defence systems. We've got hull breaches on decks two and three, emergency seals are holding, barely."

"Grant … " Diaz said flatly.

He could hear groans behind him as other members of the bridge crew regained their senses. "I can't get a report from anywhere on the ship, looks like all the comms are down. Captain, you with me?"

"She's dead, Grant."

Grant stopped and looked at Diaz, the numb shock on her face. He turned slowly.

Captain N'Koudou was still in the command chair. The stanchion above her had fallen, and had punched straight through her head and upper chest. Her blood had soaked into her immaculately pressed uniform, coating her still-twitching hands.

Grant stared at her, his mind reeling. Or'Veth and Shen'Zahr were similarly transfixed by the body. Grant had never seen an Acamar look as shaken or as horrified as they were in that moment. He blinked, and tore his eyes from the dead captain. Winters was slumped over at the helm. In the stunned silence he could make out her ragged breathing from where he stood.

He took a breath, and closed off every emotion he could. All this would have to wait. "Lieutenant Or'Veth, get me a full damage report and re-route as much power as you can to the structural integrity systems … and switch off that damn siren."

Or'Veth looked at him, and a calm descended over his face. He nodded, and sat down at the general operations station, working quickly. The emergency alarm ceased.

"Diaz, re-establish contact with the squadron and get engineering on the intercom."

She didn't answer, didn't take her eyes off the captain.

"Diaz!"

She blinked, her eyes snapping to him, anger and pain directed squarely in his direction. He'd seen enough of it from the crew of the Kodiak for it not to sting. "We need you. All of us. Take your station."

She exhaled and wiped her eyes. She sat at her station, and he squeezed her shoulder as he walked past her to the helm. As he got close to Winters, the smell of burned flesh stung his nostrils.

"Dr Shen'Zahr, I need you down here!"

Shen'Zahr ran to the helm, her medical kit in her hands. "Winters, can you hear me?"

Winters didn't react, her breathing even stayed the same.

"Lieutenant Grant, assist me. Lean her back, support her head."

Shen'Zahr and Grant took a shoulder each, and slowly lifted Winters into a sitting position. As her face caught the light, Grant tried his best not to wince.

The skin on the right side of her face was blackened and burned. Her right eye was a mess. Her throat was covered in still-smoking scorch marks. Grant supported the back of her head, her hair sticky with blood. "Come on, Winters. Ship needs her helmsman. Come on."

Shen'Zahr loaded a jet injector with adrenaline and pressed the barrel to the unburned side of her neck. She attached a set of sensors to Winters's chest and the side of her head, and her portable scanner began beeping urgently.

"Doctor?"

"If she was in sickbay …"

Grant felt his heart stop. "There has to be something …"

"She is practically brain-dead. The shock from the console, and the burns … I … "

Winters stopped breathing.

Shen'Zahr gritted her teeth and injected her again. The scanner beeped louder and louder, undeterred. The doctor send an electrical pulse into her heart, but it was no use. Winters was as stubborn in dying as she was in life, and again the high pitch whine of death filled the compartment.

Shen'Zahr removed the sensors from the body, cutting it off. The bridge went completely silent.

It was Or'Veth who broke it. "Your orders, sir?"

Grant was next in line for the captain's chair. He'd never been given command of the Kodiak, even on a night shift. Neither N'Koudou or Winters had allowed it. His prior record had haunted him the entire year he'd been aboard, coloured people's view of him, not to mention his own view of himself.

Terror started to take hold of him as he looked at the dead bodies of the captain and first officer. He wasn't ready for this. He wanted to throw up. He'd despised N'Koudou and Winters for their constant undermining of him, their backhanded remarks, their poking of the incident aboard the Berlin, the way they had spat on those that had died aboard that ship. Despite those things, he couldn't deny that they had both been good officers, good commanders, to everyone else on the ship at least.

Grant's anger at them began to grow again. Damned irresponsible, both of them, prioritising their own prejudices instead of their crew. The Free Peoples were at war. Both had to have known this could happen, and their stupidity had left him in charge with no experience for a year.

Him, whose last command decision had resulted in the deaths of four hundred people.

"Help me get them out of those chairs," Grant said to Shen'Zahr. "I don't want anyone else on the ship seeing them like this."

31

Shen'Zahr gave him a small nod as they both lifted Winters away from the helm. They started carrying her to the same corner of the bridge where White's body lay beneath a blanket.

"Diaz, have you made contact with any other ship in the squadron?"

"No," she muttered. "The comm system's fried. I've almost got the intercom back though."

"Keep at it. Or'Veth?"

"Structural integrity is holding, sir. Emergency seals are at full power."

"Good work."

Grant and Shen'Zahr put Winters down and covered her with another blanket, then turned to N'Koudou. They would have to get the stanchion loose before they could move her.

"Intercom restored," Diaz muttered.

"Call O'Hare and Holden to the bridge, then get a report from all decks, all departments. You've been at weapons before, haven't you?"

Diaz half-turned. "Yeah, I have. I've had advanced tactical training, but that was a while ago."

"That's fine. You're weapons officer until further notice."

She stared at him for a moment as he and Shen'Zahr wrenched the stanchion from N'Koudou's ruined face. "Understood," she said quietly.

Shen'Zahr's light blue skin had gone a very pale grey. Grant wiped his mouth, and held his breath as he lifted the dead captain out of her chair, carrying her to Winters and White. Diaz cleared her throat as she spoke to the department heads. Shen'Zahr covered the bodies.

"You'd better head back to sickbay, Doctor," Grant said through gritted teeth. "There'll be people there who need you. Leave them here for now."

Shen'Zahr's jaw was tight as she turned to him. "Yes, sir."

She left the bridge quickly, passing Holden and O'Hare on their way in. Both of them read the room immediately, staring at Grant. O'Hare looked at the three bodies in the corner, their blood soaking into their coverings.

"Take your stations," Grant said. "Holden, you're at communications."

Diaz moved aside to let him sit down, taking the tactical station herself. O'Hare grimaced at the smell and retched as she sat down at the helm, her eyes watering. The only one not at his station was Grant.

The command chair was soaked in N'Koudou's blood, the armrests slick with it. He stood beside it, daunted. Once he sat down, there was no going back. The ship would be his, and everything that happened from the moment his back touched the seat would be his responsibility.

"Diaz, get me sensors. I want to know exactly what's happening out there. Holden, are the deck reports in?"

"Yes, sir. We have ..." he swallowed "... thirteen dead, eighteen injured. Some of these reports are garbled, it looks like we have damage to the main computer. The FTL engine is offline, ion thrusters too."

"Life support?"

"Down on deck one. The area's sealed off, the crew in that section successfully evacuated."

Grant switched on the intercom built into the captain's chair. "Bridge to engine room. I need some good news, Mr Aarons."

There was a moment of silence. "Lieutenant Grant?"

Grant paused. "Yes, this Grant. Is that Ensign Miura?"

"Yes, sir ... Chief Aarons is dead, sir. He was killed when the hull breached. Is ... is the captain ...?"

Grant's throat caught. "Dead. Winters too, and White."

"Christ ... "

Grant closed his eyes. Aarons was one of the only people on the Kodiak who had treated him like a person, not a pariah. Diaz turned in her chair to look at him, but turned back before he could meet her eye. "Mr Miura, we're going to need the ion thrusters back online, and some power for them and the defensive systems. What do you need to make it happen?"

"Time, sir, and a dry dock."

"Moving and shooting, that's all I ask."

Miura sighed. "I'm not sure, sir. If we cut every corner and ignore safeties, three or four hours."

"I'd rather you didn't cut every corner, Mr Miura," Grant muttered. "I can divert more people your way if you need them."

"Yes sir … thank you."

Grant paused before shutting off the intercom. "You're the ranking officer on the deck?"

"Yes, sir."

"Keep your head. You've got this, Mr Miura."

There was silence from the engine room, before Miura cleared his throat. "Thank you, sir."

"Carry on." He turned off the intercom, and leaned on the captain's chair, breathing deeply. He felt completely hollow, starting to dwell on losses, his anxiety building.

"I've got partial sensors," Diaz said.

"What's the situation?"

"The Whole are ignoring us, probably prioritising ships that aren't in pieces. One of the Quinns has been destroyed. Looks like the squadron is engaging the corvettes."

"The Potemkin?"

"No change."

Grant sighed. "The Church's reinforcements will get here before The Sol Fleet do. We need to be ready for them. Or'Veth, get down to engineering and assist with the repairs."

The Acamar nodded. "Aye, sir."

"O'Hare, do we have manoeuvring thrusters?"

O'Hare checked her console. "Yes, sir."

"Set course for the nearest debris and hold position there. The more dead we look, the less tempting a target we'll be. Holden, I'll need ship to ship comms as soon as you can give them to me."

"Aye, sir."

Grant walked around to the front of the captain's chair and sat down before he could convince himself otherwise, wiping the blood from the consoles. He pressed his thumb to the intercom, broadcasting shipwide.

"Bridge to all crew, this is Lieutenant Grant. I'm sorry to report that Captain N'Koudou and Lieutenant Commander Winters have been killed in action. They, and too many others today … they were … good officers, and they were friends … and I wish we had time to grieve for them, but we don't, not now. We have a lot of work to do, we have to get the Kodiak back on her feet. There are a lot of lives on the line, not just ours."

Grant swallowed. "Do your duty, as the Captain would have expected. I have confidence in each and every one of you, because she did too, and she picked a damn good crew. Let's get to it, Grant out."

His mouth was dry. He steadied his breathing, and leaned down, wringing his hands. He glanced over at Diaz. She nodded to him, and turned back to the sensors.

3

Grant leaned over the smashed remains of the operations console and set to work on the ion engine relays. Diaz looked over her shoulder at him, stifling a yawn. She drained the last drops of her long-since cooled coffee, and attempted to rub away the headache starting to worm its way through her synapses.

They had been repairing the Kodiak for three and a half hours, picking up the pieces from the attack that had crippled them. The bodies of Captain N'koudou, Lieutenant Commander Winters and Ensign White had been moved from the bridge to the cargo bay. The sickbay morgue had already been filled by other members of the crew.

Crewman Holden glanced at her from the communications station. "Here, take my coffee. This is still my shift, technically. I'm fresh."

"Thanks, Mal," Diaz grunted. His coffee was no warmer than hers, but she sipped it gratefully. "Anything from the squadron?"

"The Arctos is on the perimeter. The Martimus and Grizzly are staying close to the Potemkin. No sign of reinforcements yet, ours or theirs." He glanced at her again. "You okay, Ro?"

Diaz sighed and rubbed her eyes. "It's … a lot."

"I hear that." Holden's console chirped. "Lieutenant Grant, message from the Potemkin. Church vessels on long range sensors. Three battle cruisers, Quinn class."

Grant turned, taking his place in the command chair. "How long have we got?"

"Nine minutes."

Grant practically punched the intercom. "Bridge to engine room. Mr Miura, we're about to have company. Give me some good news."

The engineer's voice crackled over the intercom. "We've got half power to the ion engines, another half hour will get you full. The dorsal vulcans are back to full functionality, but the ventral turrets are blind. Five of our eighteen PD lasers are running."

"Focus on those, get us up to ten if you can. I want to be ready in six minutes."

"Roger that, captain."

Everyone on the bridge froze and turned to Grant. Diaz watched him as he stared at the viewscreen, letting the comment wash over him. Slowly, he tapped on the intercom again. "I'm not the captain, Mr Miura."

"Sorry sir, old naval parlance," Miura said quietly. "The person in charge of any ship, big or small, no matter their rank … they're the captain."

Grant nodded, taking a deep breath. "Alright … carry on, Mr Miura."

"Yes sir."

Grant switched channels. "Doctor, heads up, we've got incoming."

Shen'Zahr was silent for a moment. "Understood."

Diaz caught her tone, and glanced back at Grant. Their eyes met, and he nodded to her, understanding the signal. "How are things down there, Shen'Zahr? You alright?"

"We lost Ensign Veracruz a moment ago. That makes half the crew."

Grant visibly winced. Diaz saw Holden sag beside her. Twenty three of the forty six personnel were gone. The captain, the first officer, the chief engineer … she'd worked with all twenty three for a year. She ran through the names of her friends, wondering which of them were left, a thought that no-one had time for.

"Understood, Doctor," Grant said gruffly. "I'm afraid it's not over. We've got about eight minutes until the next attack."

"Yes … sir."

Grant switched off the intercom and sighed. He paused, his eyes closed. "Lieutenant Diaz, do we have power for the rail cannons?"

Diaz checked her console. "We do."

"Good." He accessed the intercom once more. "O'Hare and Or'Veth to the bridge. All hands to battle stations."

The next few minutes passed in slow silence. O'Hare and Or'Veth walked onto the bridge and took their stations. Diaz glanced back at Grant as she readied the Kodiak's weapons systems. His eyes were closed, his chest was rising and falling rapidly. She looked at his knuckles, white as bone as he clutched the armrests.

"Grant, the defensive systems are ready," Diaz said. "Eight point defence lasers are online, the vulcans are on manual targeting."

Grant's eyes flickered over to her for a fraction of a second. "Good. Holden, where are those Quinns entering the system?"

"One eight six point two, sir, on their current course. The Arctos and Grizzly are pulling close to the Potemkin. The Martimus is heading to cover us."

"Are the Quinns in sensor range?"

Holden connected to the sensors. "They will be in about thirty seconds."

"Call the Martimus off, tell them to cover the Potemkin."

Holden turned in alarm. "Sir?"

"Do it, crewman. Bridge to engine room."

The intercom buzzed. "Miura here."

"Cut main power to everything but visual sensors, life support systems, and the thrusters."

Diaz wheeled around as Miura paused. "I can guess what you're thinking, but … they'll detect us when we power up. Their targeting sensors are quicker than ours."

"The majority of their weapons are forward facing."

Miura exhaled. "Oh boy …"

Diaz stood up. "What the hell are you thinking?"

Grant sighed. "We can't win in a head on fight with three cruisers, even with the rest of the squadron. If we play dead, and get in behind them on thrusters, we can do a lot of damage, throw them into chaos."

He was doing it again. Diaz took a slow step towards him.

He was going to get them all killed, just like the crew of the Berlin.

"Without point defence, they'll destroy us in a shot," she said hotly.

Grant looked at her. "With only eight lasers active, they could destroy us in three shots, or four if we're lucky. The ship's in pieces. Even with the squadron and the Potemkin, we can't take on three Quinns and their fighters."

"Ten seconds to sensor range," Holden said.

"You know I'm right, Diaz."

Diaz turned the pieces over in her head. There was no doubt that Ursa squadron were out-gunned, and the Potemkin was in no shape to assist in any meaningful way. The lights dimmed around them as Miura cut the power. Slowly, she sat down, turning to the viewscreen. Ahead of them, the rest of the squadron were clustered around the crippled starship, turning towards the point where The Whole's cruisers would arrive.

"O'Hare, be ready on the thrusters," Grant said quietly. He leaned forwards in the captain's chair and took out his personal transmitter. "Miura, do you read?"

"Yes, sir."

"On my signal, power up, weapons first."

"Aye."

O'Hare glanced back at Grant, meeting Diaz's eye. The young woman was sweating, nervous, breathing heavily.

"This had better work," Diaz muttered.

"You won't be around to scold me if it doesn't," Grant said quietly. "Holden, the Quinns?"

"They'd be dropping to sub-light speed in ten seconds, sir. If they spotted us …"

"I know. We'll find out very quickly."

Grant stood up and walked to the helm, leaning on the console beside O'Hare. She glanced at him, his presence not calming her in the least. He said something to her, but Diaz couldn't hear what it was. On the viewscreen, the three cruisers appeared, closing on the Potemkin. Their fighter bays opened, a great mouth on the front of each cruiser, and three squadrons of attack ships blasted out into the void.

None moved towards the Kodiak.

"They're holding course," Holden said with a gasp of relief.

The three hulking vessels drifted silently past them, their turrets aiming towards the rest of the squadron. Grant held his breath as they went, as if even a whisper would draw their attention.

"O'Hare, thrusters to full," Grant muttered. "Make it a three-second burst, we'll drift on momentum. Get us in behind them."

O'Hare took a breath. "Aye, sir," she whispered.

The Kodiak lurched as the thrusters fired, and the gunship drifted out of the debris field. There were a few pops and bangs as some of the smaller pieces of flotsam knocked against the hull.

With a succession of bright flashes, the Quinns opened fire, and the rest of Ursa squadron held position, replying with sustained bursts from their vulcans, as well as cannon slugs. The Potemkin launched torpedoes from its broadside, and fired every weapon it could muster at The Whole's forces.

The Whole's fighters dashed forwards, weaving between the three gunships. The Grizzly, Arctos and Martimus laid down a crossfire with their vulcans and point-defence lasers, catching a few of the small ships with their dense rail slugs and shattering them like shards of glass.

"Steady as she goes," Grant muttered. "Close to a thousand metres."

One of the Quinns peeled off and closed in on the Potemkin, firing its own torpedoes. The Grizzly swooped around with it, vulcans battering the cruiser's armour. The others held their position, attacking the Arctos and Martimus relentlessly. The fighters closed in on them, swarming around, focusing on their weapon emplacements. The Martimus lost its forward point defence lasers as a pair of fighters battered them, and their front armour plating was blown in half by a torpedo.

"Distance?" Grant asked tersely.

"Eleven hundred metres," O'Hare replied tersely.

"Diaz, get ready."

The Martimus was hit again, and began to drift as they lost power.

"One thousand metres!" O'Hare shouted.

Grant snapped open his transmitter. "Miura, power up, now!"

The lights on the bridge glowed dimly, and Diaz's console sputtered to life. "Weapons online."

"Tap them on the back."

Diaz practically punched the fire controls. The Quinns had the majority of their defences focused forwards, leaving the aft vulnerable. The Kodiak's heavy cannons blasted into the lead cruiser, the vulcans slicing into their engines and igniting the fuel lines. The rear of the craft exploded, sending it into a mad spin. The other cruiser began to swing around in alarm.

"Point defences to full power!" Grant ordered as he jogged back to the captain's chair. "O'Hare, ion thrusters to one half. Match the cruisers speed and put that wreckage between us and them."

O'Hare banked the Kodiak to starboard, slipping behind the wrecked Quinn. A moment later, rail-gun fire blasted straight through the stricken vessel's hull. The shots missed, but debris was propelled their way, and O'Hare had to dodge the shards of armour and hull with the manoeuvring thrusters.

"Well, nice to see they care about their crews ..." Holden said dryly.

A few fighters zipped around to target them, and Diaz signalled the vulcans, sending the tracking coordinates to them. The turrets let out short bursts, putting out a field of flak that caught a few of them.

"O'Hare, take us under the wreckage. Diaz, be ready with the heavy cannons. Keep using the vulcans to target those fighters."

Diaz signalled the gunners. As the Kodiak passed under the dead Quinn, its fusion core began to breach.

"Full speed, O'Hare," Grant ordered. Their pace increased, and Diaz compensated with the targeting sensors. As the Kodiak moved out of cover, the other Quinn stopped firing on the wreck and immediately targeted them. Miura hadn't been exaggerating about The Whole's tactical crews.

"Fire," Grant said firmly. The Kodiak's gunfire impacted the Quinn's ventral armour, but not before The Whole got a few rail shots off. The Kodiak bucked violently.

"Damage report."

"The armour's buckling," Diaz said tersely.

"Minor damage to the dorsal hull," Or'Veth said calmly. "No casualties."

Diaz watched her screens as the Arctos blasted past the Quinn, all four vulcan turrets firing. A message came into Holden's console beside her, text only.

"The Arctos just contacted us, sir," Holden said. "The Martimus is venting atmosphere. The Potemkin have a repair crew standing by for them, but they'll need a tow. Commander Xam'In says they'll cover us."

Grant nodded. "Do we have power to the grappler?"

Or'Veth checked his screens. "Yes, sir."

"Take us in, O'Hare."

The Martimus was crippled and adrift, her power fluctuating. "Full sensor scan, Or'Veth."

"The Martimus has no power to weapons or engines. Their fusion core is stable for now, but the coolant systems are damaged."

"Anything we can send over to help them out?"

"I am afraid not, Lieutenant. With the Kodiak damaged, we have no equipment of that kind to spare."

"Co-ordinate with Ensign Miura and double check. I don't like leaving them dead in the water."

"Yes, Lieutenant."

Diaz monitored her screens, watching the battle between the Arctos and the Quinn. After another attack pass by the gunship, breaching the holy vessel's defences, the cruiser came about. "Grant!"

Grant glanced at her and looked up at the viewscreen. The Quinn attacking the Potemkin and Grizzly swept around and engaged its FTL engines. Behind them, the other cruiser did the same. He raised an eyebrow and met Diaz's gaze.

"Holy shit," O'Hare muttered.

Grant blinked and let out a breath. "Come on people, let's not pop the champagne just yet. We've got a job to do. Engage the grappler, lock on to the Martimus."

Or'Veth did so, and the four grappling cables were launched, the magnetised tips clamping onto the Martimus's hull. Grant stood up as O'Hare plotted a course to the Potemkin.

"Nice flying, O'Hare," he said.

O'Hare looked around in surprise and blushed. "Thank you, sir."

"I didn't get your name … your first name."

"It's … Shelby, sir."

"Alright, Shelby. Carry on."

He approached Diaz, leaning on her console. "The course of those cruisers?"

"Back to their lines. They'll be back, and probably with company."

Grant looked up at Holden. "Any update on reinforcements from our fleet?"

"On their way, sir, but it looks like it'll be more than a day before they get here."

Grant sighed. "Alright, keep me updated." He patted Diaz on the shoulder. "Good job by the way, Lieutenant. You suit the tactical station."

Diaz glanced at him. "Thank you, sir. Can I have a word with you in private?"

Grant nodded and gestured to the corridor. "Or'Veth, you have the deck. Coordinate manocuvres with the Martimus and Potemkin. We'll be back in a moment."

Diaz and Grant stepped out into the corridor. Diaz folded her arms when he turned to her. She kept her voice down as she spoke. "That was a damn irresponsible move."

Grant sighed. "It was a gamble, yes, a gamble that ended up paying off."

"There are days where it won't, sir, you know that better than most."

Grant's jaw tightened, and his mood changed instantly. "Anything else?"

She regretted bringing up his past almost immediately. There was a flash in his eyes, the memory of his hostile year aboard the Kodiak, the aggressiveness and dismissive attitudes towards him from his peers. Given what had happened over the last few hours, it was probably all too familiar.

She softened herself a little. "Holden and O'Hare are kids. They're fresh grads, they're both enlisted crew with no officer training, they're probably not ready for this. Neither have the combat experience or training we do. I know for a fact that they haven't pulled the kind of long shift we'll be pulling here, especially not on the bridge. There's a lot riding on O'Hare especially."

Grant nodded. "I hear you, she's a little twitchy. Holden's doing alright at the moment."

"At the moment, exactly."

Grant folded his arms. "Well, they're what we have. Keep an eye on him. I'll watch O'Hare."

Diaz nodded. "Alright."

She turned to go back to the bridge.

"Lieutenant Diaz."

She stopped and turned back.

"Don't throw the Berlin in my face again. I've had enough of that bullshit for the past three years. I don't know what N'Koudou and Winters told you, and frankly, I suspect it was the same pack of lies that most people on this ship have heard. You're right about one thing, I absolutely know better than most how things can go wrong, and I'll only gamble when gambling is the only thing that might get us out of a jam."

Diaz opened her mouth to reply, but he held up a hand. "I know. It's going to be difficult to trust me. I'll have to earn it, and I plan to do so, but in the meantime we have to work together. We've got another day of this at least. For the moment, we're the two ranking officers aboard the Kodiak. That makes you the XO."

Diaz sighed. "Shen'Zahr has more experience than me. She's technically your XO, if we're going by the regs'."

"She's got enough on her plate in sickbay. You're on the bridge, you see what I see, and you're ready for the responsibility. You're the more logical choice."

Diaz remembered the conversation she'd had with N'Koudou and Winters in the mess hall, minutes before their current crisis had begun. This was a rare topic on which they and Grant would have agreed. She chose her next words as carefully as she could. "Regardless of whether or not I'm ready for it ...

I'm not going to be a good first officer to you, Grant. I don't think I can separate my feelings from my duty, especially given the circumstances."

Grant considered her words for a moment, and shrugged. "We'll see. Needs must as the Devil drives. Things are bound to change when reinforcements get here. We'll get another captain and first officer then, most likely, but right now, we're on our own."

Diaz shook her head, frustrated. "We're not on our own, Grant. The rest of the squadron have officers that could take command, or be your XO. We're just Lieutenants, there must be a Lieutenant Commander out there in the squadron, or on the Potemkin."

"Probably, but they don't know the Kodiak, or her crew. You do, and I'm not depriving another ship in the squadron of one of their officers, particularly now. You and me are our best choice, and collectively, our best chance."

"Christ ..." Diaz looked down at the deck, charred from flames and plasma burns. His logic was sound enough, in a way, but it was too much too soon.

Grant's transmitter beeped, and he activated it. "Grant here."

"Holden here, sir. I've done a little rigging on the fly and I think I've restored comms, audio only."

Grant raised an eyebrow at Diaz, who grinned tightly. "Excellent work, Mr Holden. Hail the Grizzly. We'll be there in a moment."

"Aye, sir."

Grant put his transmitter back on his belt. "Diaz, look … just think about it. Captain Latimer might agree with you, but if he doesn't, the ship's our responsibility."

Diaz sighed. "I'll think about it."

Grant nodded, and the pair returned to the bridge. Holden looked up at them as they walked through the doors.

"Channel open to the Grizzly, sir."

Grant sat in the captain's chair. "Do you read, Captain?"

Captain Latimer's gruff voice echoed over the comm system. "Who am I speaking to?"

"Lieutenant Grant, sir."

There was a moment of silence. "Captain N'Koudou?"

"KIA, sir. Winters too."

Captain Latimer said nothing for a moment. "I see. You did well in the battle. Simple tactics, but executed effectively."

"The crew know what they're doing, sir, and they do it better than most."

Latimer grunted. "N'Koudou thought the same. I'm going to miss her." He fell silent again, but only for a second or two. "That puts me in command of Ursa Squadron … and you in command of the Kodiak."

"Understood, sir."

"Has the change been noted in the ship's log?"

"It has, sir."

"Then, Mr Grant, you are hereby given the temporary rank of Commander, until the current crisis is resolved. Have your ops officer send me a status report on the Kodiak, and get your crew as rested as possible. You'll all need it."

"Yes, sir … and … thank you. I won't let you down."

There was silence again, stretching for what seemed like minutes. "Latimer, out," he finally said. The channel closed.

Diaz broke the silence first. "Congratulations … Commander."

Grant nodded to her, and activated the intercom, broadcasting shipwide. "Attention, crew of the Kodiak. Report all shift rosters to the bridge. Once that's done, Alpha shift are off duty. You've been on for more than a day, and we need you rested. You're back on at 0400."

The intercom beeped, and Grant switched over. "Go, engine room."

"Repair update, sir," Miura said tiredly.

"Go ahead."

"We can have full power to the ion engines within the hour. All four vulcan turrets should be fully operational within three."

Grant grinned, his eyes drooping. "Excellent work Mr Miura. How many of your techs are on Alpha shift?"

"Three, sir."

"Can you spare them for a few hours?"

"We'll manage, sir. Engine room out."

Grant slowly got to his feet. "Or'Veth, you have the bridge. If something goes wrong, you know where we'll be."

"Aye, Commander."

Grant hesitated before turning, meeting Diaz's eye again. "Holden, O'Hare."

Both the young crewmen turned to him.

"You've been excellent so far. Keep it up. We'll relieve you at four."

Holden nodded and smiled. "Thank you, sir."

"Thank you, sir," O'Hare repeated, shades of her nerves still creasing her brow, but not so many as there had been.

Diaz stood up with Grant, and they both left the bridge. Sleep wasn't going to come easily, even though she was exhausted. The lack of crew in the corridor chilled her to the bone. During a shift changeover, the corridors had always been full. Not now. Now, only one or two Alpha shift personnel were stumbling to their bunks, a dead look in their eyes.

Both Grant and Diaz were assigned to the same bunk room. Diaz heard Grant's bunk creak as he settled into it. She wondered what was going through his head, if he was really as confident as he seemed to the rest of the crew. She had seen the fear in his eyes.

Regardless, it was done. He was in command. The story of the EDSV Berlin echoed around Diaz's mind as she waited for sleep to come, Captain N'Koudou's words in her ear, like a lingering spectre.

"He was next in line for the big chair, so command passed to him ... but he made a mistake ..." the dead captain had said.

"He got half the crew killed."

4

"I think it's bullshit," O'Hare muttered.

Holden shrugged. "I'm just telling you what I heard, Shel'"

"Who'd you hear that from?"

"Horvath."

"The likelihood that Commander Grant traded the location of the EDSV Berlin for some kind of amnesty with The Whole is incredibly low," Or'Veth said without turning. "The likelihood is decreased significantly coming from the mouth of crewman Horvath."

O'Hare gestured to him with a thumb. "My thoughts exactly."

"You know they've got insiders in the fleet, they must do," Holden insisted. "It ain't like we're fighting aliens ... no offence Or'Veth."

"Offence is a human concept that has no place on Acamari."

"Right ... well, we're fighting other humans, and humans can be bought. That's the kind of thing The Whole do, ain't it? They worm their way into our ranks, they inform on us. You'd never know if one of them's here with us."

"He's been at the weapons for over a year," O'Hare said.

"I know ..." Holden said with a sigh.

"And we've been in how many fights?"

"I'm just saying ..."

"And I'm just saying he'd be a pretty lousy spy, blowing up his own fleet behind our gunsights."

Holden turned from his console and tapped the side of his head. "But that's the point. It's the perfect cover. You've heard about their deep-cover guys."

"The Whole prioritise victory over all else, at all costs," Or'Veth said as he stood up and moved towards the relays at the rear of the bridge. "The deaths of their soldiers are of little consequence."

"My point exactly," Holden said.

"Our vetting process is better than that, come on," O'Hare grumbled. "Now isn't the time for this BS."

"Considering your suspicious nature, it is small wonder you divide yourselves so easily, and a small wonder that agents can seed doubts within your ranks," Or'Veth said softly.

"Yeah? Well, you're stuck with us, big guy," Holden muttered.

"I would ask you not to remind me, crewman Holden."

"I'll try, Lieutenant," Holden said stonily.

"Thank you. Helm, come about to zero four five, standard perimeter patrol."

O'Hare input the course into the navigational computer. "Zero four five, confirmed."

"You gotta admit, you're curious," Holden muttered.

"No, I'm not. I'm as far from curious as anyone could get, and I doubt I'd get the truth from anyone on this ship. Everyone's got their own story, and their own version of that story." She punched in the co-ordinates and fired the thrusters. "No-one gives a shit about what really happened … they just want a version that suits them."

***

The engine room was a charred mess of burned wiring and twisted, melted bulkheads, as if it was a wax sculpture laid too close to a flame. Doctor Shen'Zahr ducked her ample height beneath a buckled stanchion, and moved through the debris.

The dwindling engineers and techs were dead eyed, drifting around like ghosts. A few of them had superficial burns that hadn't been called in. One of them, a woman no older than twenty, sat numbly, leaning against the wall next to an open maintenance hatch. The tool in her right hand was held loosely, the left singed and bloodied by flame. Her eyes were glued to a smear of dark red on the deck plate.

Shen'Zahr stooped and knelt beside her. "Are you alright?"

The engineer looked up at her. "Huh?" She looked down at the tool. "I don't ... what am I ..."

"Do not worry about that. You and I have not spoken before, have we? What is your name?"

"Pereira, Casi, Ensign, three-three-two-alpha-indigo-nine-four," she mumbled.

Shen'Zahr checked her eyes. Her pupils seemed normal, although there were clear signs of fatigue. "Are you hurt, Casi?"

"I'm ... no ... I'm just tired. You know Chief Aarons died right there?"

Her eyes had returned to the smear on the floor as Shen'Zahr began spraying a salve on the burn, preparing a set of bandages.

"Crushed when the walkway fell. Didn't see it coming."

The doctor touched her arm gently. "Should you be on duty, Casi?"

She nodded absent mindedly. "Yeah … I'm fine … I can still work … I don't want to go to bed while Takumi needs me."

Shen'Zahr nodded to her. "You are a very diligent officer, Ensign."

"Thank you, ma'am."

"Let me have a better look at your arm and give you more definitive treatment. If you want to stay, I will not stop you."

Shen'Zahr sliced Pereira's sleeve away, and applied a set of bandage seals to the burn. After, she fished into her medical kit, and pulled out two vials to load into her jet injector. She held them up in front of Pereira. "Use your best judgement. You have been on duty for nineteen hours. The shot on the left is a stimulant, the shot on the right is a tranquilliser. Takumi needs you awake and alert, but he also needs you rested."

"Awake and alert," Pereira said, eyes wide and bloodshot. "I don't want to sleep. I know what I'll see if I close my eyes … I'll see the Chief … and I don't want to be asleep when they come for us."

Shen'Zahr leaned forwards, and pressed the injector to her neck, the stimulant already loaded in. Pereira blinked as the accelerant entered her bloodstream, and took a deep breath. "Thanks, doctor."

Shen'Zahr nodded, and helped her to her feet. "Carry on."

Pereira nodded, and turned, starting to repair the conduit. Shen'Zahr kept an eye on her for a moment, before heading deeper into the compartment. Standard medical procedure had altered as desperation grew, as the war had dragged an infected every aspect of fleet operations. The engineer should really have been in sickbay, or in her berth asleep, but that wasn't how the humans did things any more.

On the other side of the compartment, where the Chief's office had been placed, Ensign Miura was wiping his brow, mapping out the repairs to the Kodiak, and what still needed doing. The schematic of the ship was almost entirely red with damaged system indicators, which was far from encouraging.

"Ensign?"

He smiled up at her tiredly. "Doc', I didn't expect to see you down here. You alright?"

"As you might say, I have been better."

He nodded, and patted her on the forearm. "I can imagine. Make sure you take care of yourself, as well as everyone else."

Shen'Zahr raised an eyebrow. "Sound advice. You should take it as well. I would advise keeping a close eye on the rest of your team in here."

"Tell me about it," he grunted. "We're going to need a week's sleep after this."

"I was thinking more about having someone to talk to."

Miura smiled tightly. "Yeah … I know. It hasn't hit me yet. I used to play poker with Pereira and the Chief. We had a game last night. We don't play for credits, thank God, or I'd have owed him a year's wages."

He shook his head. "No-one knows this engine room like he did. I've got a lot to learn."

"You have gone above and beyond so far, Takumi. You will be better than fine."

He gave her a nod, his face tight. "You been up to the bridge to see the new CO?"

"I was on the bridge when we lost Winters and the Captain."

Miura winced. "Sorry."

She waved a hand. "It is alright. Sad as it is, it is part of my duty. Lieutenant Grant seems to be doing well, considering his reputation."

"Yeah?" Miura shrugged. "That's good, I guess. I don't know … he seems like he knows what he's doing."

"I hope so. The crew is tense, even considering the situation."

Miura shrugged. "Not much we can do about it, right? Just our jobs."

"Just our jobs."

"Alright …" he reached under the console and lifted a large thermos onto the work surface nearby. "He's already had to deal with one mutiny, that's more than enough for anyone. Coffee?"

"It does not have the desired effect on Aramar, thank you." Shen'Zahr peered at him. "I have heard rumours of this mutiny amongst the nurses."

"I'm just kidding around. It's probably nothing, just tall tales."

Shen'Zahr nodded with a sigh. "I hope so."

5

The bridge was silent. Grant leaned forward in the captain's chair and focused on Diaz.

"Anything?"

Diaz switched between frequencies on the main sensor array. "They're still out there, but we keep losing the readings. Looks like they're running their jammers while operating on minimum power."

Or'Veth glanced over his shoulder. "Commander, I might be able to boost power to the sensors, with engineer Miura's assistance."

"I don't recommend that, Grant," Diaz said quickly. "For the moment, it doesn't look like The Whole know we detect them at all."

Grant scratched his chin. "Agreed. Better keep it that way for now."

Or'Veth nodded. "In that case, Commander, I recommend linking our sensors with the rest of Ursa squadron. It will be the most effective early warning system, should the vessels move in."

Grant glanced at his communications officer. "Mr Holden, do the honours."

Holden rubbed his eyes. "Yes, sir ..." he mumbled.

"Out of coffee, Mr Holden?"

"Ran out two hours ago, sir."

Grant snorted, and looked up at the helm. "How're you feeling down there?"

O'Hare grinned back at him. "I had plenty of late nights at Flight Academy, sir."

Grant raised an eyebrow. "Doing what, crewman?"

O'Hare grinned, but before she could respond, Holden piped up. "The Arctos has picked up those signals at one seven five point three, looks like they've changed course."

Grant nodded. "Match them, O'Hare. Stay in their shadow."

"Aye, sir."

Grant stood up and moved over to the tactical station. "We've been at this for an hour and a half. Any better idea of what we're actually tracking?"

"Corvettes, judging by the rough size of the signals, looks like two groups." Diaz shook her head, frustrated. "Can't tell how many of them there are, though."

Grant looked at the viewscreen. They were passing the Potemkin. The crew of the disabled battleship had been working round the clock to maintain their defensive systems, as well as repairing the Martimus, which was docked to the larger vessel's underside. "Does the Potemkin have sensors online?"

Holden sent the message, receiving a quick reply. "They're not seeing any more than we are. Captain Fairbrand is prioritising long range scans, they've got better range than we do."

"The Martimus?"

"Driver coil issues. They'll be out of the fight for at least another six hours."

Grant gritted his teeth. "Alright. Diaz, keep all the point-defence lasers online, and make sue the field of fire is as strong as you can make it on all sides. They could attack from anywhere."

The bridge doors opened, and Doctor Shen'Zahr walked in. Diaz glanced up at her and nodded. Or'Veth bowed his head towards her. Grant straightened up as he turned in the command chair. The bags under the Acamar's eyes had bags of their own, and blood had stained the front of her uniform. She was carrying a small medical case with her.

"Doctor..." he said. "How are things in sickbay?"

"Quiet … for the moment. No more losses." Her voice was flat, her words slightly slurred.

"Get some sleep, then," Diaz said. "We won't have many more moments like this."

Shen'Zahr snorted. "My nurses can sleep. I have been awake longer than this, Lieutenant Diaz. Besides, you all need to fly this crate, half of you have been on shift for around fourteen hours." She held up the case. "So I brought you some presents."

"Which are?"

She opened the case. Inside was a hypospray, with half a dozen vials of blue liquid. Grant raised an eyebrow. "Stimulants?"

Shen'Zahr grinned tiredly. "At a certain point, coffee no longer cuts the mayonnaise, Commander."

"Mustard," Diaz said with a smile.

Shen'Zahr nodded with a soft hum. "Ah. Well, it cuts neither, I am sure."

O'Hare frowned. "Are there … side effects?"

"You will break out in hives and grow a third ear. It is a stimulant, Crewman, not experimental gene therapy."

Holden rolled up his sleeve. "Stick me. The coffee on this ship's terrible anyway."

Grant grinned as Shen'Zahr administered the hypospray. "I'll make that the first item of business when we get to a drydock with a quartermaster, crewman: install a new coffee machine."

O'Hare shrugged and rolled up her sleeve. "Fine, I guess."

Shen'Zahr pressed the injector to her arm. "Let me know if that third ear starts itching."

O'Hare snorted.

"Or'Veth?"

The other Acamar didn't look up from his station. "My concentration levels are sufficient, Doctor, thank you."

Diaz rolled up her sleeve. "Go on."

"Grant?"

Grant shook his head. "Save it for Miura, I think he'll need it more than I will."

Shen'Zahr nodded. "I will. Carry on."

"Thank you Doctor, the pep up is appreciated." He stood up and walked with her to the door. "You're doing a hell of a job down there, by the way. If there's anything you need …"

"We are fine, Commander, but thank you."

Grant nodded, and Shen'Zahr left. He sighed and walked back over to the tactical console. "You didn't sleep?" he asked quietly.

Diaz glanced up at him. "Not much. Not at all, actually."

Grant sighed. "Neither did I."

An alarm went off, chirping from Diaz's console. Diaz checked her sensors. "Contacts, three Martyr Class corvettes astern!"

"O'Hare, hard to starboard!"

Grant gripped the console as the Kodiak banked, and as two rail-gun rounds slipped past the point-defence lasers, crashing against the Kodiak's aft armour. O'Hare swung the ship around, speeding towards the two ships moving in on the Potemkin. The corvettes fired torpedoes, leaving burning holes in the battleship's flank.

"You got a lock on them, Diaz?" Grant said tersely.

"Almost … wait … shit!"

The Martyrs reactivated their jammers, disappearing from the sensors. The third one caught them with another rail-gun shot, before it started to do the same.

"You're not getting off that easily," Grant muttered. "Track their trajectory, and fire the port vulcans."

Diaz carefully measured the corvette's course as it began to vanish from the screens, and signalled the turrets to fire. The port ventral turret found its mark, and there was a blast of flame and debris. Almost instantly, the Martyr shimmered back onto the scopes, and with a single shot from the heavy cannons, Diaz destroyed their command hull, fragments of deck and crew spinning wildly into the void.

"Excellent shot, Lieutenant," Grant said. "Although, they aren't usually that … squishy."

"It seems that the jamming field on the vessels draw most of the ship's power," Or'Veth said. "I would speculate that this explains why they do not fire on us while the field is active. They would have limited targeting and defensive systems."

O'Hare glanced back as she pulled the Kodiak around. "Maybe sensors too, that would explain some of their manoeuvres. They've been trying to work out if we're enemy ships or sensor ghosts."

"… without point-defence …" Diaz muttered. "Grant, I think I've got an idea."

Holden was muttering to someone over the comm system. He called back over his shoulder. "Message coming in from the Potemkin sir, audio only."

"On speakers."

Captain Fairbrand's haggard voice filled the bridge. "Kodiak, come in!"

"We're here, Captain."

"Long range sensors have picked up reinforcements from Church-controlled space. Looks like a wing of destroyers."

"How long have we got?"

"Thirty one minutes at their current speed, but they're in no hurry to get here, yet. We've got other problems. Those last torpedoes damaged our plasma coolant system. It's stable for now, mostly, but another hit could breach the fusion core."

"Understood. Kodiak out." The channel closed. "Mr Holden, contact the Arctos and the Grizzly, we need them here, now."

"Yes sir!"

"Diaz, what have you got?"

Diaz called up a tactical view of their area of the sector, and put it on the viewscreen. "There's a lot of debris in the area, small enough to not be a threat to hull integrity. If The Whole's ships move through it when they're running their jammers, they'll displace it, and I can get a target lock."

"How do we get them to fly through it?" O'Hare said.

Or'Veth highlighted a thick concentration of debris, and plotted a trajectory alongside it. "If we tow the Potemkin along this course, we can draw them in. From their view it will look as if we are preparing to flee back to our lines."

"The Grizzly and Arctos are on our wing, Commander," Holden said.

"Relay our plan to them, text only, make sure it's double encrypted."

"Aye, sir."

Grant scratched his chin. "We'll have to look like we're retreating as well, which means having our back to them … O'Hare, how fast can you pull off a hard hundred and eighty degree turn?"

"At full thrusters, from escape velocity … a few seconds. Four or five maybe." She tapped on the edge of her console. "It's not something I've tried before."

Grant grinned. "How about a spin?"

O'Hare paused. "Definitely not something I've tried before."

"We will need to boost power to the structural integrity systems, but theoretically it should work," said Or'Veth.

"Get on it, Mr Or'Veth."

"If we spin that fast, our momentum will make it nearly impossible for me to get a shot," Diaz argued.

"If I try and slow the spin with thrusters they'll probably overload." O'Hare thought for a moment. "Maybe … if I hit full burn with the ion engines at the same time, at the right moment, it should help stabilise us, but it wouldn't exactly be subtle. Even with impaired sensors, they'd see what we were doing."

"We'll have to be really quick then," Diaz muttered, relaying instructions to the gunners.

"I've been relaying to Captain Latimer, sir. He concurs with the plan," Holden said. "Squadron's ready when you are."

Grant nodded and glanced at O'Hare and Diaz. "Ready when you are, ladies."

"The corvettes have to be in the right position … hang on." Diaz focused on her tactical screens. "Signal the squadron on my mark … Now."

Holden sent the message. On the screen ahead of them, the Arctos and Grizzly fired their grapplers, locking on to the Potemkin and pulling her on a parallel course with the debris field.

"Steady as she goes," Grant muttered. "Are they taking the bait?"

Diaz's fingertips danced across the sensor controls. "I'm not sure, the debris is giving us a little interference. Trying to compensate …"

"Arctos reports that one of the enemy groups is moving to cut us off," Holden called.

"Springing a trap of their own, eh?" Grant muttered. "Are they trying to cut us off directly?"

"Yes, Lieutenant," Or'Veth said. "I have them on sensors. Logically, they will wait to attack until the group behind us open fire."

"O'Hare … reduce our speed, give them a chance to catch up."

O'Hare let out a breath, and reduced the Kodiak's speed by half. The rest of the squadron did the same.

"Got them," Diaz said. "They're moving through the debris. Target lock acquired."

Grant gripped the armrests of the captain's chair. "Distance?"

"Four thousand kilometres."

"O'Hare … ready the thrusters. Or'Veth, boost power to structural integrity. Turn on Diaz's mark."

Diaz glanced at Grant, an eyebrow raised, and he nodded to her.

"Okay …" she said, "… wait for it …"

Everyone on the bridge tensed, even Or'Veth.

"Three … two … one … mark!"

O'Hare engaged the thrusters, and the Kodiak whipped around. The hull creaked, and Grant's knuckles turned bone white. O'Hare fired the ion engines and thrusters together, speeding back towards the debris.

Grant gritted his teeth. "Fire!"

Rail slugs exploded from the Kodiak's launchers as the vulcans fired, the turrets locked onto both corvettes. One slug hit the engine pod of one of them, its fusion core igniting. Half the ship was incinerated in a bright flash, and the other Martyr-Class sputtered to a halt, its bridge destroyed and its power failing, drifting aimlessly through the debris.

Holden clapped his hand against Diaz's. "Hell of a shot, Ro."

O'Hare breathed a sigh of relief, wiping her brow.

"I couldn't agree more," Grant said with a grin. "And that was some fine flying, O'Hare."

"Thank you, sir."

Grant took a breath. "Okay … bring us about. Diaz, the rest of the squadron?"

Diaz glanced at her screens. "Giving them both barrels, Commander."

Grant grinned. "On screen."

The Grizzly and Arctos were swooping around one of the Martyrs, finishing it off with their vulcans. Another had been disabled, and the Potemkin's rail-guns had made short work of a third.

"Let's join the party, O'Hare. Full burn."

The final Martyr fired on the Arctos as it sped between the frigates, heading back towards The Whole's territory. They engaged their FTL engines, and blasted away.

"Track them, Diaz," Grant said. "Holden, status report from the fleet?"

"The Potemkin and Grizzly are undamaged, the Arctos's armour is holding. The Potemkin's hailing us."

"Put them on screen."

Captain Fairbrand appeared on screen, a little bedraggled, exhausted, but standing with her back straight. "Excellent work, Commander."

Grant glanced at Diaz. "Actually, it wasn't my idea, Captain, I owe my tactical officer and helmsman a beer. How are things over there?"

"We're held together with tape and good wishes, but we're more or less stable. Hold on, we're linking the squadron into this transmission..."

The screen divided into four, and three faces joined Fairbrand's. Captain Latimer nodded to everyone, eyes lingering on Grant. Commander Xam'In of the Arctos appeared beside him, her bone white skin contrasting her black eyes. Commander Yin'Vas of the Martimus had a deep, wicked-looking cut across his forehead.

"We've got good news and bad news for you, Ursa Squadron," Fairbrand said. "Bad news first. That corvette is heading towards the incoming destroyers and they've increased speed. They'll be here in about seven minutes. The good news is, Sol Fleet reinforcements will be here in five. Ursa Squadron are hereby relieved, and ordered to Drydock 27 for repair and resupply."

Tiredness and relief seemed to wash over everyone on the bridge like a wave. Grant looked at the other COs of Ursa Squadron. They seemed to feel the same way. Latimer closed his eyes and nodded. Yin'Vas slumped, staring into space. Xam'In sighed shakily.

"If it's all the same, Captain Fairbrand, we'll wait until our ships get here," Grant said quietly. "Just to be safe."

The other captains nodded their agreement.

"We appreciate it, Commander," Fairbrand replied. "We'd also appreciate a tow to three two mark six, if you don't mind."

Latimer grunted. "Kodiak, you fly cover, we'll handle the tow."

"Yes, sir," Grant said, and the channel closed. "O'Hare, set course."

O'Hare did so in silence.

"It's hard to believe …" Diaz muttered.

"We'll pull off plenty more miracles, Lieutenant Diaz," Grant said. "Especially with this crew."

Nice words. Well deserved, considering that the bridge crew had had around eight hours of sleep between them over the last three days. Still, they felt as hollow as his temporary rank, which would most likely be stripped from him the second the Kodiak docked.

Probably for the best. Grant hadn't earned command, not by a long way. He'd paid dues, but not the ones he needed to. He'd been flying by the seat of his pants, carried by Diaz, Miura, Shen'Zahr and the rest of the crew.

They weren't even his crew, they were N'Koudou's. Given her animosity towards him … not only could he not afford to not be perfect, but even if he never made a mistake, there was no guarantee that he would be accepted.

Lucky. That's all he was. Maybe he was due some luck, but still, it would run out eventually.

What happened aboard the EDSV Berlin had left a sizeable scar on his confidence, on his reputation. He would likely still be a pariah, no matter what he did, no matter how many dues he paid.

He banished the last thought with a grunt. Self pity didn't serve anybody.

"Our ships are coming in, Commander," Diaz said.

Grant looked up at her. He'd forgotten where he was for a moment. "Yes, right. How many?"

"Seven. Two repair tugs, plus the Gaddesden, the Patton, the Endeavour, the Markland and the Nagasaki."

The ships slowed to sub-light speed and took up defensive positions. Two were Hammer-Class destroyers, two were Drake-Class light cruisers, and one was a Wyvern-Class frigate, leading the task force. The tugs swept forwards and locked on to the Potemkin and the Martimus, readying them for FTL travel.

Holden's console chirped. "The Nagasaki's hailing us, Commander. Admiral Valiente."

Grant straightened up in the command chair. "Put her on."

Valiente's stern face appeared on the viewscreen. She looked like a hawk, her fierce gaze piercing into Grant. One of her eyes had been replaced by a prosthesis, blacker than the void itself. Her hair was cropped to an inch in length at most.

"Where's Captain N'Koudou?" she asked.

"She was killed in action, Admiral."

Valiente glanced at the data-pad in her hand, skimming the report. "Why was The Fleet Admiralty not informed of the change in command?"

"I don't know, Admiral. We've been under heavy fire, and when we haven't, time has been taken up with repairs. Some of our official duties have been less pressing. I apologise for not notifying you sooner, although the change has been noted in the ship's log."

Valiente nodded. "It's understandable. According to this report, you've been at this for three days."

"Yes ma'am."

"Good job, Mr Grant."

Grant tried not to fall out of his chair in shock. The last time Valiente had spoken to him was as one of the judges at his court martial, and she had condemned him as a coward, who had brought shame to the uniform.

He swallowed. "Thank you Admiral."

"Head for Drydock 27. Ursa Squadron have earned a little shore leave. I'll debrief you on this incident in two days, when reinforcements arrive. Now, if you'll excuse me, there are zealots on our doorstep."

"Give them our warmest welcome, Admiral. Good luck."

Valiente nodded, and the channel closed. Grant pressed the intercom. "Mr Miura, can you give me FTL speed?"

"Yes sir, but no more than factor two, I'm afraid."

"Suits me fine. O'Hare, set course for Drydock 27."

"Aye, sir," she said.

The stars turned blue, then violet on the viewscreen as the Kodiak accelerated to faster-than-light speed. A moment later they disappeared entirely into the ultraviolet spectrum, and the void began glowing blue as the background radiation of space became visible. Slowly, the blue glow focused and warped into a cone, stretching out in front of the ship.

Normally, the blue-shifting of space at faster-than-light speed was magnetic, hypnotic even, the transition breathtaking. At that moment, Grant found little enjoyment in it. His eyes were drooping. He stifled a yawn.

His thumb found the intercom once again. "Crew of the Kodiak, this is acting Commander Grant. You've gone above and beyond the call of duty over the last few days, and ... those we've lost would be proud of you. We'll have a little shore leave at Drydock 27, and you've more than earned it." He paused for a moment, gathering his thoughts. "I'm not sure what happens next. I don't know who will command this ship when repairs are complete ... but I know you'll do them proud as well."

The bridge crew had all watched him speak. He looked at them, their fatigue, their determination, their relief, their sadness. Diaz smiled at him sadly, a smile he returned. O'Hare and Holden both nodded to him. Or'Veth slowly turned back to his readouts, monitoring the power levels.

Time to arrival at Drydock 27?"

O'Hare ran the numbers quickly. "Eleven hours, present speed."

"You and Holden have earned a break, I think. Go get some sleep."

Holden snorted. "With those stimulants, I don't think I'll be sleeping anytime soon. Thanks anyway, Commander."

"I've got a few hours left in me, sir," O'Hare said with a grin.

"Or'Veth?"

The Acamar turned to him. "I will meditate for an hour, then return to duty. If I may say so, Commander …"

"Go on."

"You mentioned to Lieutenant Diaz earlier that neither of you got much sleep during your off-hours."

Grant smiled to himself and closed his eyes. "And you think that we should take a break."

"It would be a wise course of action."

Grant glanced at Diaz, who grunted. "I'm not about to argue with a Acamar after a 72 hour shift."

Grant laughed. "Neither am I. Go and meditate, Or'Veth. When you come back, you have the bridge."

"Aye, sir." Grant took his seat at the operations console.

"After all that, we'd better be getting medals," Holden grumbled to himself.

"Can't argue with that, Mr Holden." Grant smiled at the readouts. All the power levels were firmly in the green. "Maintain course, O'Hare. We've got backs that need patting, and Drydock 27 has beer that needs drinking."

6

Grant opened his eyes, jogged from sleep by Crewman Upworth

as he jumped off the last rung of the ladder that led up to his bunk. He stretched and grunted at the stiffness in his back, a long running side-effect of having to sleep on a prison mattress, even though it had been a few years since his release.

At least there hadn't been any dreams, sheer exhaustion had drugged his imagination into a brief comatose state. Such deep sleep was a rare pleasure. Grant checked the shipboard time on the bunk room wall. 14:12. He'd missed his alarm.

He glanced across the bunk room. Diaz was zipping up her uniform, the navy blue jumpsuit they were all made to wear. She grunted at him as he dragged himself out of bed.

"Coffee before we get to drydock?" he asked.

"I'll take it on the bridge," Diaz muttered. "Better make sure O'Hare hasn't fallen asleep at the wheel." She sighed and rubbed her head. "No matter how much sleep you have after a long shift, it never feels like enough."

"I'll bring a flask up." Grant rubbed his eyes. "Tell me the showers are working now, at least."

"They're working. I can't vouch for the warmth of the water."

"I'll see you on the bridge then. When are we due in drydock?"

"15:09."

"Alright," Grant said, grabbing his towel from the drawer that held his meagre belongings. "I'll be there in twenty minutes."

He spent almost all of those twenty minutes in the lukewarm shower, washing off three days worth of body odour, sweat, blood and grime. His shoulder ached incessantly, Doctor Shen'Zahr's temporary treatment of it starting to wear off. He would have to have it checked at the station.

He pulled on his uniform and made his way to the mess hall, his shoulder protesting during the climb down the access ladder to deck three. He filled a large thermos with the hot mud that passed for coffee on the Kodiak, and stopped by sickbay on the way to the bridge.

Doctor Shen'Zahr looked up at him as he entered the cramped compartment. The beds were in the process of being cleaned, Nurses Langer and Ther'Iyn sterilising them with fine lasers. The room still stank regardless.

Twenty three of the Kodiak's crew had died, some of them in here, and the recycled air had grown stale, like an abattoir that had been abandoned.

"Your shoulder?" the doctor asked.

"Yeah, I think I slept on it. You guys want coffee in here?"

Nurse Ther'Iyn turned around. "By the Scholars, yes." Langer nodded with a forced smile.

Grant smiled as he poured three cups with the hand that wasn't occupied by Shen'Zahr. She injected a painkiller into his bicep, and massaged his shoulder muscles gently with her long, thin fingers.

"We're sterilising and charging our equipment," Shen'Zahr said. "So the painkiller and massage is going to have to do for the moment."

"I'm not complaining, doc'. Look, we'll be in drydock for at least a week, according to Miura. Take that week as shore leave, head down to the planet and get some fresh air."

"Are there beaches on Arcturus Prime?" Ther'Iyn wondered.

"Absolutely," Langer said.

Shen'Zahr rolled her eyes. "Alright, although if I can get a shuttle to one of the poles, I cannot guarantee I will come back …"

His treatment finished, he strode out and up the corridor, past the crew quarters to the bridge, where his makeshift senior crew were waiting.

When the doors opened, he could already see that Crewmen Holden and O'Hare were flagging. The two junior officers had been awake for more than a day. Or'Veth was as unflappable as ever, and Diaz was leaning over him, checking the power relays.

"I know it's terrible, but who wants coffee?" Grant asked with a grin.

Holden groaned. "I could drink that entire thermos, sir."

"I'll bet. O'Hare?"

"Absolutely," she grunted from the helm.

"I already have a spiced tea, thank you, Commander," Or'Veth said.

"Make it a double for me," muttered Diaz.

Grant brought cups to each of his officers, and sat in the command chair. "Anything to report?"

"Repairs are progressing steadily on all ships in Ursa Squadron, Commander," Holden said between sips. "The Potemkin reports that their reactor coolant system has been repaired. Captain Latimer has called for all commanding officers to meet for debriefing at zero nine hundred hours tomorrow."

Grant sighed. The last thing he wanted to do was re-live the last three days. The deaths of the captain and first officer, the chief engineer, and so many others, hung over the Kodiak. The ship felt empty, hollow, with fresh scars outside and in.

Grant activated the intercom. "Bridge to engine room."

"Miura here, sir."

"How are the engines looking?"

"Well … I don't want to risk repairs while we're at FTL. Things are still a little shaky, but I'll be honest with you, sir, they could be a lot worse."

Grant raised an eyebrow. "I was hoping for some more … encouraging news, Mr Miura."

"We've done all we can down here sir. We're not miracle workers. The best I can say is that we're not in danger of bursting into flame."

"I'll take that. We're due at the bar when we dock, and I owe you a few drinks. Up for it?"

"Always, Commander."

"Good man, bridge out."

O'Hare piped up from the helm. "Approaching Arcturus Prime, sir."

Grant grinned. "Speaking of which … slow to sub-light speed. All stations, prepare for docking."

The stars rushed back into view, as did the planet, Arcturus Prime. The Arcturus system was highly disputed between the Free Peoples and The Church Of The Whole, and had been for decades even before the Interstellar Holy War. The surface of the planet was scarred from dozens of engagements, orbital bombardments, and the skeletons of crashed starships.

Drydock 27 was the latest in a series of outposts that had risen and fallen over the years, and was certainly the hardiest of them. The large orb-like hull that held the main hub of recreation, crew, laboratories, machine shops, repair bays and other amenities sprouted eight docking arms, like a large, metal octopus in space. The surface was covered by point defence laser turrets, as well as hundreds of more powerful anti-ship batteries. A number of Sol Fleet and Acamar military starships were orbiting the station, and even more were docked for repairs.

Holden activated the Kodiak's transmitter. "Drydock 27 docking control, this is the EDSV Kodiak of Ursa Patrol Squadron, registry two seven four delta, requesting permission to dock for repairs." There was a pause as the reply came through his earpiece. "We have permission, Commander. Docking berth eighty."

"Thank you. Take us in, O'Hare, manoeuvring thrusters only."

The Kodiak flew in, the rest of the squadron splitting off towards their own berths. As O'Hare slipped the gunship beneath one of the docking arms, Grant caught a glimpse of two ships attached to the same structure they were heading towards. One was a Challenger Class cruiser, the registry EDSV 71α emblazoned across its flank. The Yamato, if he remembered correctly. The other ship he recognised immediately, a Nevada Class heavy cruiser he was all too familiar with.

The Berlin.

Diaz seemed to recognise the ship as well, and in his peripheral vision he saw her turn in her seat to face him.

Hell, most of the Kodiak's crew probably recognised that damn ship.

Kodiak 1: Trial By Fire

O'Hare slowed the Kodiak, lining her up with the drydock arms. The docking clamps closed around them in a tight embrace, and airlock gantry stretched out to meet their own umbilical, attaching with a loud click. "Docking complete, Commander," she said.

For a moment, Grant didn't answer. Diaz stood up. "You okay, Grant?"

"I'm fine." Grant beat the screaming past into silence as he stood up shakily and pressed the intercom. "All crew, shifts are suspended until further notice. Enjoy your shore leave, you deserve it. Engine room, if you haven't done so already, please submit a status report to the dry dock repair crews."

He looked around as the bridge crew hauled themselves to their feet. He unhooked the personal transmitter from his belt. "Miura, Shen'Zahr, meet us at the airlock. I hope one of you knows a place to get a decent drink on this tub."

***

As it turned out, Shen'Zahr did.

Cadman's Pride And Joy was a dive bar that had been set up in a disused cargo bay. Grant had heard of the place in passing, but it seemed his CMO had been a regular when she had served in the Acamari Guard.

The bar was quiet, but there was roughly an hour to go before shifts aboard the drydock changed. A model of the ESV 1, humanity's first faster-than-light starship, stood on the shelf next to a multitude of liquor bottles.

"No knock-offs here," the bartender said proudly. He was a Styj, as broad as he was tall, like a great hairy sphere with warm eyes and a toothy grin. His arms rubbed his ample girth with a jolly zest. "What'll it be?"

Grant decided on what the bartender claimed was genuine New Orleans bourbon, a double shot on the rocks for each of them. A pricey choice, but this was meant to be a celebration.

"You'd never guess how damn difficult it was getting these off Earth," the Styj muttered as he poured. "Plenty of smugglers were locked up or worse, trying to get people and goods away. Real tragedy. Those people are heroes."

"*They're* the heroes, huh?" Holden grumbled.

"More for the people, less for the bourbon," Grant muttered.

"Right," Holden said. "Guess there are a lot of people trapped on Earth, huh?"

"We may be fighting against Earth, but Earth was the first planet The Whole conquered," Diaz grunted.

Holden nodded. "I guess so. I hadn't thought about it that way."

Or'Veth smelled the contents of his glass, raising an eyebrow. "This beverage will have no intoxicating effect on me, Commander."

"Do not be so sure," Shen'Zahr muttered "I have made that mistake many times with the human beverage 'tequila'."

"Think of it as a human ritual," Grant said. Diaz smiled to herself.

"I think I have tried this before," Shen'Zahr murmured. "I think ... nights here are often a blur."

Grant held up his glass, and the rest did the same. "To the crew of the Kodiak. Those that are here, and those that can't be."

The glasses clinked together, and they drank. Warmth filled Grant immediately, and despite it he shivered with satisfaction. Diaz closed her eyes, swallowing the bourbon with a sigh. "I'd forgotten what that tasted like ..."

O'Hare coughed, drawing a grin from Miura. "Not your speed, Shel'?"

"I'm more of a cocktail girl," she croaked.

Holden laughed. "We've got a few days here, and I can't help but notice the variety of booze on offer. I bet that bartender could make a mean Long Island ... "

O'Hare grinned. "You're on. Ro?"

Diaz grinned. "Can't pass that up."

Miura shook his head. "I'd love to, but I want to give them a hand fixing up the Kodiak. We cut a lot of corners, and I don't want the techs getting confused."

Grant gave a mock gasp of indignation. "You are on shore leave, Mr Miura. I'm mortified."

"No rest for the wicked, Commander."

"Well, cheers to you," Shen'Zahr said. "For holding our girl together."

"Hear, hear," Grant agreed, holding his glass out to him.

Miura grinned and looked down. "I'm filling big shoes, gotta do them proud."

Grant's smile faltered a little at the memory of Chief Aarons. "You're filling them and then some, Takumi. He'd be proud of you."

Miura looked up and nodded, appreciating the sentiment. "Well, I'd have a lot more pieces to pick up if the ladies at the wheel and the guns weren't so good at dodging and blasting every zealot in sight."

Holden clinked glasses with O'Hare and Diaz. "Damn right."

Or'Veth observed them all quietly, bemused. "This is a most confusing human ritual. It seems to entail drinking alcohol and aggressively complementing one another."

"Someone is feeling left out," Shen'Zahr said with a smirk.

Miura raised his glass. "To our operations officer, who doesn't sleep, apparently, but can still wire a console better than some of my engineers who are fresh on-shift."

Or'Veth stared at them, waiting.

"Raise your glass, and say 'cheers'," Grant whispered. Or'Veth raised his glass, and the crew raised theirs.

"Cheers."

Shen'Zahr laughed quietly, shaking her head. "You will get used to it."

"How did you even find this place?" Diaz asked her.

"When you are on an Acamari Guard ship in this area of space, you get familiar with every establishment that sells Glacier Ale."

"Sounds like our second round of drinks," Holden said with a grin.

"As your CMO, I should probably protest that very loudly..." Shen'Zahr muttered.

"Is it safe for humans?" O'Hare asked carefully.

Shen'Zahr grinned. "Define 'safe'."

Grant snorted. "It's happening, everyone in?"

"Good lord..." Diaz muttered. "Fine."

"I'll probably regret it, but I'm in," Miura chuckled.

The rest nodded their agreement. Or'Veth cocked his head to the side quizzically. "Is drinking potentially dangerous fluids also part of the ritual?"

"Absolutely," Shen'Zahr laughed. "Just ... refrain from drinking it chilled. Seriously. Mine and Or'Veth's systems can take it, but I have treated enough frostbite for one lifetime ... "

Grant looked at Holden and O'Hare. "We'll need them. Holden, O'Hare, both of you have gone above and beyond, when the Kodiak needed you the most. I spoke to Captain Latimer earlier, and he agreed with me. He also sanctioned this ..."

Grant fished into his pockets, and placed two rank pips on the table. Holden and O'Hare stared at them. "You're officers. Congratulations."

O'Hare looked up at him. "I ... Commander ..."

"You've both more than proved yourselves."

"Oh man..." Holden muttered, picking up his pip. "I don't ... know what to say, sir ... "

"You don't have to say anything. I'm not about to take the pips back if you don't make a good enough speech." Grant raised his glass, the last sip of bourbon. "To Ensign Malcolm Holden, and Ensign Shelby O'Hare."

Diaz patted Holden on the back. "Well deserved."

"Damn, I hope so. Thank you, sir."

"Speaking of something being well deserved ..." Grant withdrew another rank pin, this one for a lieutenant. He placed it on the table, and slid it across to Miura. " ... I can't think of a better option for chief engineer, not on the Kodiak, not in the squadron."

Miura stared at the pin, and slowly attached it to his uniform. He cleared his throat. "Thank you, Commander. I'll ... do my best. It's a lot to live up to."

Or'Veth bowed his head towards him, and Shen'Zahr patted him on the chest with a broad smile. "You are up to the challenge, and I doubt anyone on the Kodiak would doubt that."

Grant nodded to him and smiled. "Not a chance. Now, on to the next round. Glacier Ales, coming up."

"Not chilled," Shen'Zahr said sharply. "Seriously."

Grant winked at her, and walked over to the bar. A moment after he had ordered the ales, O'Hare sat beside him on one of the raised stools. "I won't let you down, Commander, I swear."

"I know, that's why I gave you the pip. Relax, Shelby. We're on shore leave."

She grinned. "My mum's going to want to speak to you, when she hears about this. She always does. I think she's still on a first name basis with all of my professors at the Academy."

Grant raised an eyebrow. "Why's that?"

O'Hare shrugged. "I guess she just likes to know I'm in good hands."

"Well, I hope she approves."

"She will." O'Hare looked at the pip in her hand, turning it over with her fingertips. "I used to dream about flying a starship. Dodging asteroids, diving through nebulae, looping between the stars. It's … hard to believe it's actually happening. I just … I wish it happened differently … you know?"

Grant squeezed her shoulder. "I know, but we play the hands we're dealt as best we can. You're a gifted pilot, and I can't think of another person I'd want at the helm. Whether it's me who takes command of the Kodiak, or someone else … you'll do them and Winters proud."

O'Hare looked up at him and smiled sadly. "Thank you, Commander. That means a lot."

As Grant and O'Hare waited at the bar, there was a commotion at the doorway. A large group of Sol Fleet officers had walked in, loud and raucous. The bartender waved to them. "More of the Free People's finest gracing my establishment. What are you having?"

"Half-litre ales, all round, on their XO."

Grant froze at the voice as the rest of the newcomers cheered. He turned slowly as he heard the footsteps behind him falter and stop.

Commander Jan Nevin stared at him in disbelief.

Fury rose in Grant immediately. His fists clenched. O'Hare looked at him, alarmed.

Jan kept her face as neutral as she could. "You got out."

"Eighteen months ago, Commander." He couldn't help but spit that last word, despite himself.

Jan's eyes flickered to O'Hare. "Girlfriend?"

O'Hare frowned. "Helmsman. Who are you supposed to be?"

Nevin straightened up. "Is that how you speak to a superior officer, Ensign?"

"Courtesy isn't one-way, Commander Nevin, not for most people," Grant snapped. "If you'll excuse us …"

Grant and O'Hare picked up their round of drinks. O'Hare looked slightly alarmed at the blue, almost luminous liquid they were about to drink as they started to walk back to their table.

"Orson …" Jan said.

Grant stopped walking, but didn't turn back to her.

"I'm glad you … I'm glad you're out. It's good to see you back in a uniform."

Grant didn't give her a chance to say any more. He kept walking, rejoining his crew. O'Hare sat down, eyeing him curiously. "Who was that?"

"Old friend."

"Didn't seem like she was a friend."

Diaz glanced up, looking at the insignia of the crewmen who had just entered. Her eyes darkened. "They're from the Berlin."

O'Hare's mouth closed. "Oh."

Grant swallowed. "'Oh' is putting it mildly, Ensign."

"She said, 'you got out'. Out of where?"

"The NZ2 Penal Colony. Prison."

O'Hare's eyes widened, and she looked away. Someone clapped Grant on the back. "You're him, right?"

Diaz and Holden stood up. Grant turned around. A group of four were standing behind him, all enlisted crewmen. One of them, a woman, nodded. "That's him."

Grant stood up slowly. "Now is the wrong time for this. Step back."

"No, I don't think so." The woman's hands balled into fists. "I know a lot of people who aren't alive today because of you."

"Back off, crewman," Diaz said firmly, standing beside Grant. "That's an order."

The fracas was beginning to draw the attention of more of the Berlin's crew. "Lafferty!" Commander Nevin shouted. "Stand down!"

Lafferty bared her teeth. "You should have died with them, you son of a bitch."

"Lafferty!"

The crewman glanced at Nevin, and took half a step back. Grant saw through the feint, and sure enough, she lunged forward, aiming a punch at him.

He ducked the blow, and pushed her away. "I said, not now, damn it!"

The crewman who had clapped Grant on the back raised a fist, and Or'Veth immediately grabbed his forearm, restraining him with a gentle hand on the shoulder. The man struggled a little, but couldn't escape the Acamar's grip. Shen'Zahr and Holden circled round the table as more of the Berlin's crew began advancing on them.

Grant glanced around him as Miura and O'Hare got to their feet. Diaz had her fists balled up, ready for whatever would be thrown at her. Shen'Zahr calmly circled around Or'Veth, whirling and kicking Lafferty squarely in the jaw as she came at Grant again with two others. The shock of that allowed Grant to move in and shove one of the men back. The other caught him with a punch that rattled across his forehead. He returned the favour, jabbing him in the solar plexus, upper-cutting him under the chin.

An officer's whistle screeched from the doorway. Everyone in the room immediately snapped to attention.

"Senior officers, step forward."

The voice was calm, but firm at the same time. Grant and Nevin stepped from the crowd and stood to attention in front of the three people who had just entered. One was a woman, a Commander, tall and slender, her dark hair cascading over her shoulders. Standing beside her was an Acamar, watching them like a school principal. In front of them was a man in his early sixties, his expression stern. He was a Captain, and a seasoned one at that.

"Commander Nevin, there are better ways to blow off steam," the man said.

"Yes, sir."

"So … who started the fight?"

Nevin said nothing. The Captain looked at Grant. "Well?"

"My presence instigated the fight, Captain, I accept the blame."

The Acamar frowned. "Your presence instigated the fight, but you did not start the fight? A most curious situation."

"It was one of my crew, sir," Nevin said. "Captain Delyle and I will deal with the matter."

Captain Delyle. Grant's lip threatened to curl, but he kept his face straight. For her to be made captain … and captain of the Berlin in particular …

It was almost too much. He seethed quietly, trying not to let it show. The Acamar fixed his eyes on him, a stare that made it clear that some sign of pain had gotten through.

The Captain nodded to Nevin. "See that you do." He raised his voice to address the room. "Save it for The Whole! I don't know what your issue is, and I don't care! You're officers of the Sol Fleet, not first year Academy cadets in a downtown Arcturus bar. You may be free people, but the fleet expects better of you. Understood?"

The room replied in unison. "Yes, sir!"

The Captain turned to Nevin. "Commander, take your people to another bar. There's one you'll enjoy three decks down on the promenade."

"Understood, sir. Move out, people!"

The Berlin crew filed out, glaring at Grant's officers. A few still looked like they would make a move for him, but with the Captain and his command crew there, they didn't dare. The Captain walked to a table in the corner with his companions and beckoned Grant over.

Grant glanced at his people. "Everyone alright?"

They nodded. Diaz took a drink of the Glacier Ale, not meeting his eye. He knew what she was thinking. *Will this happen every time? Will they turn on me, because of the pariah on our ship?*

Grant sighed and walked to the Captain's table. The bartender had left the same bottle of bourbon that the Kodiak crew had drunk from earlier in front of him.

"Someone's been at the damn liquor ..." the Captain muttered.

Grant coughed. "That was us, sir. Sorry."

His superior grunted. "Well, at least you've got some taste."

"At least you didn't break any of the furniture," the female Commander muttered. "I assume there was some reason a new front in the war almost broke out in here?"

"An ... old reason, ma'am."

"Is that so?" the Captain said. "We haven't met before. I'm Captain

Yari Cifarelli, EDSV Yamato. This is Commander Robbins, and Commander El'Zin."

"Acting Commander Orson Grant, sir. Ursa Squadron, Kodiak, two seven four Delta."

"Ah …" El'Zin and Robbins exchanged a look as Cifarelli poured four glasses of bourbon. "Old reason indeed. That explains the bar fight, then. You look like you need a drink, Mr Grant."

"I appreciate it, Captain."

"Just an acting Commander?" Robbins asked.

Grant nodded and sighed. "Our CO and XO were killed in action. Captain Latimer granted me the rank temporarily."

"Kodiak … Ursa Squadron... You were under the command of Captain N'Koudou."

"Yes, Commander, we were."

Robbins nodded. "I'm sorry for your loss."

"Thank you. It's a … it's hard, as you can imagine, for the rest of the crew more than me."

El'Zin frowned. "How so?"

"This … bar brawl … I've been dealing with attitudes like this for a year. People drag me and my name through the mud constantly, and the fact that these people were from …" He trailed off, staring into his bourbon.

"The EDSV Berlin," the Acamar finished.

"Yes sir."

El'Zin raised an eyebrow. "Most fascinating. The incident aboard the Berlin was six years and four months ago. It is illogical to judge an officer on an event so far in the past, particularly considering the war."

"We're not the most logical species, El'Zin," Cifarelli said as he passed him a glass of bourbon.

"Yes, Captain, we have noticed."

Cifarelli gave him a wry smile. "Time is relative, isn't it. An event six and a half years ago may be distant for you, but for other people it might as well have been yesterday. I imagine that's how it feels for you sometimes, Mr Grant."

Grant took a long drink of bourbon. "You're not wrong, sir."

"I've read the initial reports of your defence and rescue of the Potemkin. Three days of fighting, feeding on adrenaline and luck, repairing your ship on the fly without any sleep ... I've been there. It's enough to break even the most experienced officers, but it seems like you did a good job."

"My crew deserve most of the credit, Captain."

"Maybe so, but if you keep it up, that's what you'll be judged on, not the Berlin."

Grant looked at his hands. "Judging by the way people have treated me, including Captain N'Koudou, I don't think I'll be given the chance, sir."

"Then take it when it presents itself. Make yourself undeniable, Mr Grant. You're living in your past just as much as the rest of them, shake it off, and earn your chance if it won't be given. Beg, steal or borrow it, and work harder than you did the day before until you're where you want to be." Cifarelli leaned back, peering at Grant closely. "Even the deepest wounds need a chance to heal. Seems like you're so busy pouring salt on them yourself you're getting in your own way."

Grant sipped the bourbon. Maybe he was living too long in his past, but being reminded of it constantly didn't help. "I don't know sir. I'll try."

"That's a start. Less brawls in future as well, Mr Grant. A wiser man once said to turn the other cheek, and he didn't just say it because it sounded nice. Now, you'd better get back to your crew before they pass out. Looks like they've been through hell."

"Aye Captain. Thank you."

"Best way to thank me is by proving your doubters wrong, Mr Grant. Seems like you're doing a fair job so far, if the report I read is anything to go by. Bar fight notwithstanding."

"I will, sir. Commander Robbins, Commander El'Zin, good to meet you."

Robbins nodded. "Likewise."

He walked back towards the Kodiak crew, Cifarelli's words buzzing through his head. The veteran captain was probably right about him, although Grant didn't know how he could put them into action. He didn't even know whether he would still be on the Kodiak after Admiral Valiente had debriefed him.

That was one thing that had settled in his mind.

The Kodiak was where he wanted to be, he was sure of it: aboard that tiny, cramped starship, with its hard beds, bad coffee and unappetizing rations, despite the sour memories he'd had during his service there. One look at the crew as he rejoined them at the table told him that.

He didn't want to leave them, not after the battle that had brought them together.

Grant sipped his Glacier ale. It had an aromatic sourness to it, the alcohol in it noticeable but not overpowering.

"You okay, Grant?" Diaz asked.

He was silent for a moment. "No, but … I think I will be, and that's better than I was yesterday."

7

Diaz pressed the door chime, preparing herself for what lay beyond the threshold. She had been asked here out of the blue, and had assumed it was some kind of meeting for the senior officers of Ursa Squadron. However, Grant hadn't known anything about it, and even though she was on time, she was here alone.

"Come in," Captain Latimer's gruff voice said from the other side of the door.

Díaz opened the door and stepped inside. The room was an officer's lounge, offering a stunning view of Arcturus Prime. A huge electrical storm was settling over the northern continent, bolts of lightning slicing through the clouds to and fro, like there was a battle raging in the heavens.

Latimer, Commander Zax'In and Commander Yin'Vas were sitting on a pair of couches, stacks of reports on the coffee table in front of them. Even though it had been three days since Ursa Squadron had docked at Drydock 27, all three still looked exhausted. Diaz imagined she looked no better.

"Lieutenant Diaz, reporting as ordered."

"At ease, Lieutenant," Latimer grunted. "Repairs to Ursa Squadron are progressing well, we're just waiting on the Martimus, and on the replacement crewmen. I understand you need quite a few aboard the Kodiak."

Diaz twitched at the comment. "Yes, sir."

Latimer sighed gruffly. "I'm sorry, Lieutenant, I know how that sounded ... but I have to think about these things now. I understand that Lieutenant Grant has filled out the senior staff."

"He has, sir. He notified you, I believe."

"He did. Commander Zax'In?"

Zax'In picked up one of the information pads on the table. "Ensign Shelby O'Hare has been assigned to the helm, is that correct?"

"Yes, ma'am."

Zax'In nodded. "... and Ensign Malcolm Holden to communications."

"And Lieutenant Takumi Miura has been promoted to chief engineer, yes ma'am," Diaz said.

Zax'In looked up at her, frowning. "And you to tactical."

"Yes, ma'am."

Zax'In leaned back, studying Diaz carefully. "We're concerned, Lieutenant, about the experience of these officers, yourself included."

"I have full tactical training, ma'am."

"O'Hare is a year out of the Leonis Flight Academy, Holden fifteen months out of Zosma Basic. Miura has never been in any kind of leadership position, and you may have training, Lieutenant, but you have only completed three shifts at tactical."

"Four, technically ma'am, if you count our recent battle."

Zax'In threw the pad down on the table. "Not enough. For any of you."

"With all due respect, ma'am, I'm not sure what you expect me to do about that."

"Be objective, and honest, Lieutenant," Latimer said. "Grant has made poor decisions, objectively, in his choice of senior officers."

He caught Diaz's frown and held up a hand. "That's not a slight against you, don't get me wrong. You're a good officer, I have plenty of reports from your former captain and instructors that tell me that."

"With all due respect, Captain, it may not be a slight against me, but it is a slight against Holden, O'Hare and Miura. Understandable, but you've seen their work first hand. We wouldn't have survived without them. May I ask a question, sir?"

Latimer settled back into the sofa, and nodded. "Please do."

"Why are you not referring to him as Commander Grant? His temporary rank hasn't been rescinded yet."

Latimer sighed and looked at Zax'In. "It will be. The transfer order Captain N'Koudou put in has been forwarded to Admiral Valiente. He will likely be on his way back to Leonis Spacedock for reassignment before the day is out."

"N'Koudou's dead," Diaz said flatly. "Besides, if it weren't for Grant, we'd all be in the same state. His plan, and those new officers, allowed us to beat back three cruisers, and more besides."

"Grant's plan got a quarter of my crew killed and crippled my ship, Lieutenant," Yin'Vas said quietly. "There was a better way."

Diaz's temper flared. "Then someone should have executed that theoretically better plan, Commander, with all due respect. Grant might be … unconventional, but …"

"What you call unconventional, I call irresponsible," Yin'Vas hissed.

Diaz almost bit back, but resisted the urge. "I would have too, before I saw him in action. What you were questioning was his officer assignments, and clearly O'Hare, Miura and Holden have proved themselves to him. They've proved themselves to me as well as XO, and they must have had some impact on you, because during the defence of the Potemkin you went along with two of the plans we formulated, both of which worked with minimal loss of life."

"On your ship, maybe," Yin'Vas growled.

"That's enough, Commander," Latimer admonished quickly. He turned back to Diaz. "Admiral Valiente will be arriving on the Nagasaki within the hour. If I were you, Lieutenant, I'd prepare myself for some changes. Now that I'm in command of Ursa Squadron, there will be far less gambling with the lives of our people, particularly with Orson Grant off the Kodiak."

"Sir … "

"Dismissed."

Diaz's lip curled. "Sir …"

"Dismissed, Lieutenant," Latimer said firmly.

Diaz clenched her teeth and turned on her heel, marching from the room. It was too much to bear, the deaths of her friends, the breakup of the crew. Her eyes were watering, and she wiped them angrily. She pulled out her personal transmitter, trying to think of who she could talk to about this. Shen'Zahr was on the planet, relaxing at the southern pole. Miura was assisting with repairs to the Kodiak. Holden and O'Hare would likely be hungover …

She activated it. "Diaz to Or'Veth."

After a moment, the Acamar replied. "Go ahead, Lieutenant."

"Do you have a moment?"

"I am on my way to a tea house on deck one of the promenade. Would you care to join me?"

Diaz sighed. "I'd like that, yes. I need to talk about something, and you're the coolest head I know."

"I am at your disposal. I will send the location of the tea house to your transmitter."

***

Or'Veth sipped his spice tea as he listened to Diaz recount the meeting with the COs. "It seems the animosity toward Commander Grant stretches further than the Berlin and the Kodiak."

"Well," Diaz said, "I doubt there's much animosity towards him now on our ship."

Or'Veth's head bobbed thoughtfully. "It would be preferable to think so, but I am not sure. If I may, humans have an illogical obsession with past mistakes."

"We judge people on patterns of behaviour," Diaz said. "But sometimes something big enough happens, and it tends to blow everything else away."

"The incident aboard the EDSV Berlin is synonymous with Commander Grant. It must be incredibly difficult for him."

Diaz sighed with a shake of her head. "You were his relief, right? Never on the same shift?"

"Indeed."

"Captain N'Koudou and Lieutenant Commander Winters were … outright hostile towards him at times. People kept their distance from him … I kept my distance from him, even though I didn't have much of a problem with him most of the time … but when it's your Captain and one of your friends doing it constantly … and there's the things you hear … y'know?"

Or'Veth cocked his head to the side slowly. "I do not."

Diaz sighed and sipped her tea. The spice in hers was said to be mild, but a large enough sip made her tongue go numb. "I was friends with Winters, good friends … and we … I'd hear things, see her attitude towards Grant. There are times when I look at him … and I see what she saw, I remember the rumours about him, and … I don't know."

"I am not sure what you want me to say."

Diaz looked up at him. "I'm not sure either."

Or'Veth sighed as he put down his mug of tea. "The Admiral's decision is final. If she decides to reassign Commander Grant, that is her prerogative. She will have listened to the other commanding officers' concerns, no doubt. It is a complicated decision."

"I don't envy her, either."

"The Acamar do not envy, Lieutenant. I am simply pointing out the multitude of variables involved."

Diaz sighed. "What do you think?"

Or'Veth raised an eyebrow, and sipped his tea once more. "I do not have a 'problem' with Commander Grant, or his record. Rumours and hearsay do not concern me. His command decisions thus far have been sound, and he seems to care for the lives and well-being of those under him. If reports of the EDSV Berlin incident are accurate, he has seen first hand how grave mistakes can be. It follows that they are not mistakes he will repeat."

Diaz frowned. "What do you mean, '*if* they're accurate'?"

"Following the trouble in the bar, I took the liberty of examining the Fleet's archives on the Berlin incident. Several of the statements are contradictory, based on evidence that is, at best, circumstantial."

Diaz put down her mug and leaned forwards. "What about Grant's testimony?"

"The blame, according to then-Lieutenant Grant, lay with then-Lieutenant Nevin, and then-Commander Delyle."

"The captain and first officer of the Berlin?"

"Yes. At the time, Delyle was executive officer aboard the EDSV Venture, the other vessel involved in the incident, which was also destroyed by the same assailants that attacked the Berlin. Do you wish me to forward the reports to you?"

Diaz almost said yes, but … "No, that's alright. Honestly … I don't want to even think about it. I want to judge him for what he does, not what he did, if that makes sense."

"It makes perfect sense, Lieutenant."

Diaz grinned to herself. "Thank you."

She raised her mug, and Or'Veth knocked his own mug against it. "Cheers."

Diaz smiled and shook her head. Out of the window to her left, a ship slowed to sublight speed, appearing between blinks. She was a Wyvern Class frigate. She narrowed her eyes at the registry as it flew closer.

It was the EDSV Nagasaki. Admiral Valiente had returned.

***

Grant took a deep breath and pressed the door chime. He had watched the starships zipping back and forth around the docking arms, as he had when he was a child on his father's cargo hauler, watched the maintenance pods buzzing around the Kodiak with fresh hull and armour plates clutched in their tiny claws. He had hoped it would calm his nerves, but it hadn't at all, and when he saw the Nagasaki dock, his heart had leapt into his throat.

"Come in."

Grant opened the door and stepped into the office. Admiral Valiente was sitting behind a large, mahogany desk, that stuck out like a sore thumb in the modern looking office.

"Have a seat, Mr Grant."

"Yes, ma'am." Grant settled in the chair opposite her. "How are things out there?"

"We brushed aside that wing of destroyers without too much trouble. We tangled with a few Quinns as well, but managed to fight them off. We'll be establishing a forward outpost in the debris field, an early warning system for when The Whole move on Arcturus. Ursa Squadron and the EDSV Potemkin are to be commended for your role in establishing a foothold in the system."

"Just doing our job, Admiral."

"Hmm." Valiente pressed a thumb to a small control panel by her hand, and a screen rose from a slot in the desk. "I'm told there was some excitement in Cadman's Pride And Joy the other night."

Grant coughed. "You could say that, Admiral. Not the finest hour for those involved, myself included."

"Coming from you, that's quite the statement."

Grant raised an eyebrow. He hadn't expected a jab this early. "Well, I didn't start it."

"You didn't finish it, either. You have to be more responsible than that, if you're fit to command a starship, even if it is just a gunship." Valiente pressed a button, and a hologram appeared in the air between them, a database running down his recent record. "Although, it isn't exactly surprising, given your history aboard said gunship. Insubordination, dereliction of duty, insubordination again, and again, and again..."

Grant raised an eyebrow. "Pardon me, ma'am … dereliction of duty? That one passed me by …"

Valiente glared at him, touching another button. One of the segments in the database expanded into a report. "You refused to attack a supply ship, on its way to Procyon."

Grant grunted and shook his head. He might have guessed. "Ah. Yes. I didn't want to alert their escorts to our presence. They were running active jammers, I spotted the signs. We were outnumbered three to one, and Captain N'Koudou refused to listen. She ordered the Arctos to fire when I wouldn't. Naturally, we were seen, and the squadron was forced to retreat. We lost eight crew, the Arctos lost nine."

"Captain N'Koudou's report says differently."

Grant raised his hands with a shrug. "I'm not surprised, Admiral."

Valiente closed the report. "You are a royal pain in the ass, Lieutenant."

"Yes, ma'am, so I'm told."

She stood and began to pace. "You should be a Commander by now, at least, and I mean a real Commander, not the temporary rank you've been given, which is hereby rescinded."

Grant nodded. Not unexpected.

"If you just reigned in your damn mouth, you'd have a lot more friends in the fleet. You've been assigned to ship after ship, and it's been the same story every time. The CO puts in a transfer request before you've been aboard for two weeks, and you move on."

"With all due respect, Admiral, what do you expect me to say? 'I'm sorry'?"

"I don't know at this point. It's frustrating. You're clearly talented. Some of the aptitude you've shown at tactical is inspired, but you don't show it nearly often enough."

Grant sighed. "I suppose not, ma'am."

"Don't you have anything to say in your defence?"

"No, ma'am. Whenever I defend myself, it seems it's written up as insubordination. Besides, with all due respect, it's getting tiresome having to explain my past to deaf ears. I'd rather just get on with my job, but there are times I try to do that and it gets thrown in my face."

He relaxed his posture and began to pace, shaking his head. "That dereliction of duty note in my record is a joke ... it's the duty of the chief weapons officer to make a tactical assessment of a situation, and report that to the captain. It's not my job to tell them what they want to hear. I've had commanding officers that want a yes-man, like N'Koudou did. Just' 'shut up and do what I tell you.' People who played ball did well under her command, people like Winters and White, and even ..." He hesitated for a moment. "Even Diaz, in some ways."

"Then maybe, Mr Grant, you should start playing ball."

"Not when lives are at stake, Admiral. Especially not in war." Grant sighed. "If I may ask, Admiral, what's all this about?"

Valiente smiled tightly and stepped over to the coffee dispenser in the corner. "Black, dash of caramel, dash of salt. Something interesting landed on my desk while the Nag' was out with the battle group. It was passed on via a couple of other pen-pushers. Apparently, Captain N'Koudou requested you be transferred off the Kodiak, effective immediately should the Kodiak return to a port."

Even though she was dead, N'Koudou was still lingering to haunt him. Grant sagged. "Of course she did," he muttered.

"A request I'm throwing out."

Grant straightened up. "What?"

"I've been through the report of your defence of the Potemkin, as well as Ursa Squadron's and the Kodiak's logs. You did well."

"I ... um ... "

Valiente sat back down with her coffee. "This war is chewing us up, Grant. Attrition is taking its toll. We're losing a lot of good officers, and too many leaders. There have been some questions raised, and frankly I have some myself, but without you in command of the Kodiak we would have lost Ursa Squadron and the Potemkin. There's no doubt about that."

Valiente opened a drawer in her desk, and placed a ranking pip on the table. "Too many of us are starting to get weak chins, or they're starting to give up on the idea that we could get the zealots out of our lives permanently. We need more commanders who can think outside the box and get things done. You've got a lot of potential. I want you to know that, and I want you to get your head out of your ass, because you're about to have a whole lot more riding on you, and you know the consequences when things go badly."

"I ... Yes ma'am."

"Stop calling me 'ma'am'. 'Ma'am' is for useless people."

Grant steadied himself and nodded. "Understood, Admiral."

"Better. There are people in Ursa Squadron who aren't going to like this. I'm expecting a few calls, but it's your job to prove them wrong, Lieutenant Commander."

The Admiral stood up, and Grant followed suit. He didn't know what to do, didn't know what to say. Valiente walked around the desk and pinned the new rank to the patch over his heart. "Congratulations, Mr Grant."

"I … you …" Grant took a breath, trying to stop his throat closing. "Thank you, Admiral. I won't let you down."

She shook his hand. "No, I don't think you will. The Kodiak is yours, Lieutenant Commander Grant. Take care of her."

8

The Kodiak was bustling with activity. Diaz and Shen'Zahr edged along the corridor, dodging technicians and engineers as they tinkered with the wiring and power conduits in the walls. The floor was a mess of coffee cups and tools, circuits and broken parts. The ship was supposed to be ready to depart the station the next day, but it seemed like half of it still needed to be put back together.

"I do not envy Takumi," Shen'Zahr muttered. "The ship is a mess."

"Hmm," Diaz grunted.

"Are you alright, Ro?"

She wasn't. Not in the least. "Let's just get this done."

They climbed up to deck two, which was in even worse shape than three. At the end of the corridor, it looked like the bridge was being completely rebuilt. Half the helm console was being carried away, and the chairs were sitting in the corridor in a row. It looked as if they had been cleaned.

Two doors up from the ladder, to Diaz and Shen'Zahr's left, was where they needed to go. Diaz's fingers hovered over the controls, and she had to take a deep breath before opening them. Shen'Zahr squeezed her shoulder.

"Come on. Better not put it off any longer."

Diaz nodded, and opened the door.

Lieutenant Commander Winters's quarters were a mess. The gravity plating must have failed at some point during the battle with The Whole. Her possessions were scattered all over the floor, her bedclothes strewn haphazardly.

"I will get a packing crate from the cargo bay," Shen'Zahr said. "Are you going be alright?"

"Yeah, go on. I'll make a start."

Shen'Zahr left the room. Diaz took a deep breath and started picking up a few things, putting them on the bed.

The first was a guitar. The body had been cracked and the two top strings had come loose. Winters had been learning to play it, she'd shown Diaz, Shen'Zahr and a few others after a few beers too many on Hastings Colony in Denebola. They had ended up singing old songs from Earth and Acamari until the early hours of the morning, when Captain N'Koudou had knocked on the door and ordered them to bed.

There were pictures on the floor, the frames broken. One was of Winters and her sister, from when they were recent graduates from Leonis Academy. Another was taken on Paradia, an oceanic world in 55 Cancri, Winters frolicking on the beach with a group of friends. Another was of her looking at the Kodiak, from the observation platform at Leonis Spacedock.

She had been so proud to serve aboard the Kodiak, so proud to be first officer to Captain N'Koudou. She had been a damn good helmsman, compassionate, cocksure of course ... but she'd been a good friend. Someone to talk to, someone to look up to, even. She hadn't been perfect, her attitude towards people had made Diaz uncomfortable at times, and when she thought she was right, she could be stubborn as a mule.

Diaz sat down on the bed heavily, the last picture in her hand. It hadn't had a chance to sink in, there hadn't been a moment where grief could really take hold, but now ...

The Kodiak would depart Drydock 27 without Winters, without Captain N'Koudou, without Chief Aarons, without Ensign White. Half the crew would be strangers.

Shen'Zahr walked back into the room, collapsible crate under her arm. When she saw Diaz, she sighed and put it down by the door, sitting beside her.

"It's never been like this ..." Diaz muttered. "We got lucky so many times, we came out of fights bruised, people ... people lived."

"No, people died ..." Shen'Zahr said flatly. "Forty seven, before last week. I called time of death on all of them. Fourteen engineers, fifteen technicians, sixteen security officers, and two of my nurses."

Diaz sighed and wiped her eyes. "God … I'm sorry … I just …"

"It has never been so many at once."

Diaz said nothing. If it were anyone but the ship's doctor, she might have gotten away with her feelings without confronting them at all.

"*I* got lucky," she murmured bitterly. "Not '*we*', *I* got lucky."

Shen'Zahr didn't reply.

"In this whole war, on my tours of duty, I hadn't lost anyone. I didn't really know the crewmen we lost before. I've lost people I'd met here and there, old acquaintances, but … no friends, no family. Never lost a Captain." Tears began running from her eyes. "So god-damn selfish …"

Shen'Zahr took her hand. "You cannot know what you have never faced. I have a few years on you, and it still stings every time you lose someone. I lost more in the Acamari Guard … hundreds more even. Still, not much has hit harder than this." She looked down, her head drooping. "It is different on a small ship. You get to know every face, every name, where they come from, who they really are. Some … some of them were so young … full of gusto and dreams, wanting to defend their colonies, defend freedom itself …"

Shen'Zahr closed her eyes. Diaz squeezed her thin, pale hand. "We'll give people that chance."

The doctor smiled sadly. "We could all die tomorrow, Rosario. The Whole could come to Drydock 27 in force and vaporise everyone and everything. In our next battle, we could get hit even worse than before."

"We can do something about the last one, hopefully."

"Hmm …" Shen'Zahr chuckled. "That is going to depend on our new Commanding Officer …"

Diaz nodded and sighed. Since Grant's promotion to Lieutenant Commander, he had fallen almost completely silent. He had spoken to her once, sending her a list of possible candidates for new crewmen, very no-nonsense, very little excitement or happiness in his voice. "Have you seen him since he spoke to Admiral Valiente?"

"Briefly. He sent me some personnel files, he wants to add another three nurses to my staff. I know what happened on the Berlin … happened, but I think we could be in good hands."

Diaz nodded. "Yeah, I think so too. It's … strange."

"What is?"

"That he seems to suit it so well, even though …"

"Because he has paid the price already," Shen'Zahr said. "He does not want to pay it again. His time aboard the Kodiak has not been easy, and it will be a lot harder now. What is the problem?"

"I don't know … I'm just … worried about him, I think. I'm worried that people are going to be weird about following his orders. There are still people aboard who don't exactly like him."

"They will do their duty," Shen'Zahr said. "And if they do not, there are always other ships they can serve on."

"But during a battle …"

"Then we have a brig," Shen'Zahr said bluntly. "But I do not think it will be an issue. Grant has thick skin, after what happened to him. He served under Captain N'Koudou without many complaints."

"Then where the hell is he?" Diaz said. "We all lost people in that battle, the changes on this ship are going to be tough for everyone."

Shen'Zahr raised an eyebrow. "Computer, locate Lieutenant Commander Grant."

A mechanical voice buzzed from the intercom: "Lieutenant Commander Grant is in his quarters."

Shen'Zahr grinned. "The engineers installed a vocal input on the main computer yesterday."

"Interesting voice. Kind of … motherly."

"Only if your mother has an iron throat." Shen'Zahr looked at Diaz. "If you have concerns, address them. You know where he is."

***

Once Winters' possessions were packed, and on their way to Leonis, Diaz made her way to the captain's quarters. They were on the same deck as hers, the opposite side of the corridor.

She pressed the door chime. There was no answer from beyond the threshold. After a few moments, she pressed it again.

"Come in."

Grant's voice was tired, haggard. Diaz opened the door and stepped inside. N'Koudou's quarters were a couple of feet wider than the XO's berth, with a desk beside the window. They were more Spartan than Winters' had been, it seemed Grant had already cleaned it out.

He was sitting at the desk, staring out at the stars. He glanced at Diaz, and softened a little. "Sorry about that, I was miles away."

"You alright, Grant?"

"Just … busy."

His desk was empty, aside from a couple of report pads. The one in front of him was on, displaying a personnel report.

"Am I disturbing you?"

He was silent for a moment. "No, come in. Help yourself to a coffee, N'Koudou had a pretty excellent machine installed. I was thinking about having Miura put it in the mess hall."

He gestured to a recessed panel set into the wall, with a little black shelf the precise size to hold a mug. Diaz ordered a black coffee, and drank in the rich, roasted smell of it as the liquid poured into a mug. She sipped it, and sighed like it was her first drink of water after a day in the desert

"If you installed this in the mess, you'd have the whole crew petitioning the Admiralty to make you a Captain," Diaz muttered.

Grant snorted. "Sure."

Diaz sat on the edge of the desk. "Are you really alright?"

"I'm having some trouble with old ghosts." He sighed. "Honestly … I'm terrified."

"Of what?"

"Of screwing up, of things not going our way, of people … relying on me. I don't think I'm ready for this."

Diaz leaned forward. "You got promoted, and given a command, because you are absolutely ready for this. You proved that. Come on, Grant."

"I … shit, Diaz." He looked down. "I've been looking through personnel reports, getting the crew together … and with the war … some of them are probably going to die. I'm sick of people dying under my command. I've got enough blood on my hands."

"You haven't lost anyone on the Kodiak yet. Don't be an idiot."

Grant glanced at her with an eyebrow raised. "That should be 'don't be an idiot, sir.'"

Diaz half smiled. "What's really wrong? You took to command without a second thought. You changed an Admiral's mind. You changed my mind, Grant. If you were really so dead set against having the responsibility of the Kodiak, you would've told Valiente, or resigned your commission. It's not as if the fleet has been good to you over the last few years."

She paused before saying what she'd been about to say. "If this is about the Berlin …"

Grant put the report in his hand down on the table with a clatter. "People keep telling me to forget it … move on. They're right … of course they're right, but …"

"No 'but'. You have a ship. If you can't move on now, you never will."

Grant sighed. "I've always wanted to be the captain of a starship, since I was a boy. I used to read about fighters like Valiente, and explorers like Captain Ricardo and Captain Stewart. I've got my wish … I thought I never would, when I was in prison. I thought my chance had gone. Now, it has happened. Here I am, and I can't look at myself in the mirror because it's been … beaten into me that I don't deserve it."

He looked around the room. "It's hard, being in here. These are my quarters now, and I don't even have the stuff to fill two drawers. If N'Koudou were still alive, I'd be stuck on the station." He punched in a code into a control panel on the desk, and a screen extended from it, lighting up with a list of files.

"All her logs were still in the computer. It's almost like she'll walk in any second. I feel like … an imposter, wearing someone else's clothes, in someone else's life. I'm going to have to go above and beyond to earn it, and I won't have any excuses any more. I won't have anyone to blame, except myself, because the buck stops right here, with me."

Diaz folded her arms. "You seem to blame yourself for a lot of things, Grant."

He spread his hands. "When your mistake leads to the deaths of a few hundred people, you find a lot of blame."

Diaz looked at her feet. "You're putting a lot of pressure on yourself, a lot more than anyone else is."

"Well … it's not something I want to happen again …"

"You really think it would?"

Grant looked at her and leaned back in his chair. He picked up the pad that was sitting on the desk.

"I don't know. I guess I just have to try my best, and hope I chose a good crew." He waved the pad. "N'Koudou left this on, seems she was halfway through a log before something interrupted her. There were some … colourful words said about me …"

Diaz sighed. "You know what? If N'Koudou and Winters were alive, they wouldn't be denying what you did in the captain's chair. Pretty sure they'd be proud of you."

"Maybe. We'll never know, now. What was more interesting to me is what they said about you."

Diaz frowned. "What?"

"Apparently, she and Winters were going to make you second officer."

She sighed. "Yeah … I know. They told me just before we picked up the Potemkin's distress call, but it was between me, Shen'Zahr and Aarons."

"I'll do you one better."

Diaz shook her head. "I told you, I won't be a good first officer to you."

"You already have been."

"Grant, you have access to dozens of Lieutenants on Drydock 27 who've been waiting for a chance, their personnel files are a button push away."

Grant shook his head. "They'll get their chance, I'm sure. I want someone I trust, someone who can see things that I don't see. I want someone the crew trusts and respects. There's no-one better than you, at least not for me."

"Shen'Zahr."

"She's a better fit for second officer. I want my XO on the bridge. She recommended you, by the way, and she isn't the only one."

"Grant …"

"Computer, play final personal log, time index two, eleven, zero."

N'Koudou's voice appeared on the intercom, and I haz got to her feet, startled. "… when we've finished our last patrol. Winters and I have been talking about the second officer position, and neither of us have a better recommendation than Lieutenant Diaz. She's damn good, well liked amongst the crew, and she'll go far."

Diaz stared at Grant, who smiled at her sadly.

N'Koudou continued: "I just wish she had a little more … I don't know. I wish she knew how good she was. I wish she had the confidence to be who she could be. That'll come with time, and maybe a few knocks, but we both have every confidence in her. She's more than ready, and she'll make a hell of a captain when her time comes."

Diaz felt a lump form in her throat. Grant stood up and walked around the desk, placing his hands gently on her shoulders.

"I know you can do this, Ro. If you don't believe me, believe the Captain. She chose you for a reason, the same reason I'm choosing you now. There's no-one else I'd want watching my back, no-one else I'd want in that chair if I couldn't be."

Diaz took a deep breath and looked up at Grant. "Who are we to argue with Captain N'Koudou?"

"As someone who argued with her a lot, I wouldn't recommend it. It gets to be a real pain in the ass."

Diaz grinned. "Thank you … I won't let you down."

Grant took her hand, and shook it with a nod. "Neither will I."

***

Grant sat in the captain's chair, and took a deep breath. "Clear all moorings."

"Aye, sir," Or'Veth said, working his controls.

"O'Hare, thrusters to half power until we're clear of the docking births, then pull us into formation with the rest of the squadron."

"Yes, sir."

Holden turned in his chair. "Orders are in from the Grizzly, sir. Our patrol route is at two three zero mark five."

"Course set, sir," O'Hare said.

Grant pressed his thumb against the intercom. "Mr Miura, are we ready for FTL?"

"Yes sir, full power at your command."

"Good man."

The bridge door opened behind him, and Shen'Zahr entered, a soft smile on her face.

"Everything alright, Doctor?"

"Just here to see us off, sir."

Grant smiled. "Wouldn't have it any other way."

He looked past her at Diaz, who glanced back with a grin. "All decks report ready, sir. The Arctos is on our wing. Ready for you to give the word."

Grant took a deep breath, looking around at the crew one more time. Or'Veth was patiently waiting for the order. Holden was monitoring communications between the ships of Ursa Squadron. O'Hare was positively glowing, adjusting the Kodiak's position with tiny bursts from the thrusters. Shen'Zahr and Diaz were watching him, smiling.

"Let's not keep The Whole waiting. Take us to FTL, O'Hare."

The Kodiak will return in

#2 Dance With The Devil

coming soon ...

Printed in Great Britain
by Amazon